They were standing so close that she could smell the scent of his cologne, and it was going to her head.

And there were those eyes of his....

Sky-blue and looking down at her with something that might have been interpreted as appreciation, if she didn't know that was crazy.

He's just being friendly.

I'm pregnant.

He's not going to kiss me....

And yet...

He also wasn't making any move to leave. Or to take his hand away from her arm. Or even to stop that tiny massage of his thumb that seemed increasingly like more than support or comfort.

And he was studying her with an intensity that seemed more than friendly.

Was she imagining it because she wanted it to be true? Because she wanted him to kiss her?

Dear Reader,

Issa McKendrick has moved back to her hometown of Northbridge, Montana, with a secret. The end of her last relationship left her with a little surprise—she's pregnant. That relationship is one-hundred-percent over and done with. But she's decided to have the baby, despite the fact that doing it on her own is a daunting prospect.

Former football star Hutch Kincaid has moved to Northbridge to raise his toddler son and to mend fences with his twin brother. He's been widowed for a year and a half but he's not in the market for a new woman in his life, or in the life of his son.

But in comes Issa anyway. And while a baby fathered by someone else has to be one of the biggest obstacles there is, somehow not even that can keep these two apart.

Or can it?

I hope you enjoy finding out!

Best wishes,

Victoria Pade

MOMMY IN THE MAKING

VICTORIA PADE

Harlequin®

SPECIAL EDITION

Recycling programs
for this product may
not exist in your area.

ISBN-13: 978-0-373-65644-8

MOMMY IN THE MAKING

Books by Victoria Pade

Harlequin Special Edition

¤¤*Fortune Found* #2119
***Big Sky Bride, Be Mine!* #2133
***Mommy in the Making* #2162

Silhouette Special Edition

Willow in Bloom #1490
*Her Baby Secret #1503
*Maybe My Baby #1515
**The Baby Surprise* #1544
His Pretend Fiancée #1564
***Babies in the Bargain* #1623
**Wedding Willies #1628
***Having the Bachelor's
    Baby* #1658
‡‡*The Pregnancy Project* #1711
¤*The Baby Deal* #1742
***Celebrity Bachelor* #1760
***Back in the Bachelor's Arms* #1771
***It Takes a Family* #1783
***Hometown Cinderella* #1804
**Bachelor No More #1849
¶*A Family for the Holidays* #1861
***The Doctor Next Door* #1883
††*Designs on the Doctor* #1915
***Hometown Sweetheart* #1929
***A Baby for the Bachelor* #1971
‡*Texas Cinderella* #1993
***The Bachelor's
    Northbridge Bride* #2020

***Marrying the
    Northbridge Nanny* #2037
***The Bachelor, the Baby and
    the Beauty* #2062
***The Bachelor's
    Christmas Bride* #2085

Silhouette Books

World's Most Eligible Bachelors
Wyoming Wrangler

Montana Mavericks:
    Wed in Whitehorn
The Marriage Bargain

The Coltons
From Boss to Bridegroom

*Baby Times Three
**Northbridge Nuptials
‡‡Most Likely To…
¤Family Business
¶Montana Mavericks:
    Striking It Rich
††Back in Business
‡The Foleys and the McCords
¤¤The Fortunes of Texas:
    Lost…and Found

VICTORIA PADE

is a *USA TODAY* bestselling author of numerous romance novels. She has two beautiful and talented daughters— Cori and Erin—and is a native of Colorado, where she lives and writes. A devoted chocolate lover, she's in search of the perfect chocolate-chip-cookie recipe. For information about her latest and upcoming releases, and to find recipes for some of the decadent desserts her characters enjoy, log on to www.vikkipade.com.

Chapter One

"**A**sh! Asher! Get back here!"

A man's voice.

Whispering.

Something about ashes?

Coming out of a sound sleep, Issa McKendrick's first thought was that she was dreaming.

Until, very near to her ear, she heard, "Pit-tee."

Pity?

Struggling out of heavy slumber, she opened sleep-bleary eyes.

Staring at her almost nose-to-nose was a very small boy.

"Hi!" he greeted her happily.

"I'm sorry."

A man's voice again, this time not whispering, coming from the door to her apartment. The door that was wide open.

From her position lying on the sofa, Issa bolted upright, alarmed by the fact that she wasn't alone. That a strange man and child were there.

"Get back here, Ash," the man repeated more firmly.

"Bye," the child said before he did as he'd been told.

Issa's vision was beginning to focus as her gaze followed the child and landed on the man.

Whoa!

Dreamy-looking guy—maybe this *was* a dream....

"I didn't mean to just come in," he said then, convincing her with the deep tones of an intensely masculine voice that she was awake. "I'm Hutch Kincaid, your landlord..."

Hutch Kincaid.

Still trying to get her bearings, Issa was not quick on the uptake. It took her a moment to put things together in her mind.

Hutch Kincaid *was* the owner of the house-turned-duplex where Issa had an apartment on the upper floor. Her brother had rented it for her when she'd announced that she was moving back to her hometown of Northbridge, Montana and wanted a temporary place while she looked for a property to buy.

Hutch lived in the lower half of the building, but he'd been out of town when Issa had arrived two days ago, so they'd yet to meet.

"I got the note you left under my door downstairs and you're right," he was saying when she began to gather her wits, "this lock is broken—all I did was knock and the door opened. And then Ash barged in before I could grab him."

Issa took in the view of the man standing in her doorway.

He was very real and very good-looking. Big and strapping, with an athlete's broad chest and shoulders, a narrow waist and long legs all barely contained in jeans and a lime-green polo shirt.

And the face—sharp jawline; longish, thin, somewhat pointy nose; just-full-enough lips; the sexiest dip in the center of his chin; and eyes the blue of a cloudless summer sky. Top it all off with short, sunkissed sandy-brown hair worn with the top a hint longer and carelessly disheveled, and he was quite a sight to wake up to.

"It's okay," Issa finally said. Her voice was groggy and small. She was embarrassed to be caught sleeping in the middle of a Sunday afternoon. "Come in."

That was as much invitation as the little boy needed—he promptly left Hutch Kincaid's side and came back to the sofa as Issa pivoted to put her feet on the floor.

Her intention had been to stand to greet her guests and hopefully regain some of her dignity.

But it didn't take more than that pivot to make her so dizzy that she couldn't get up as the room seemed to spin around her.

"Just a minute…" she muttered, further embarrassed and feeling as if she were making a spectacle of herself. "I'm really light-headed all of a sudden…"

"Take your time," Hutch Kincaid urged as his jeans-clad legs came into her wobbly view in the center of the room, on the opposite side of the coffee table.

The coffee table where she had a number of illustrated pamphlets in plain sight, all titled things like *Pregnancy and You, So You're Going to Have a Baby* and *What to Do Now that You're Pregnant…*.

Dead giveaways.

Of the biggest secret Issa had ever kept and the one most important to her not to let out.

Any hope she might have had of Hutch Kincaid not becoming aware of the pamphlets evaporated when the little boy pointed them out with a chubby index finger and said, "Bay-bees."

"Why don't you come over here with me, buddy," Hutch Kincaid suggested.

"No. Pit-tee."

The little boy couldn't possibly know that she was pregnant, that she was horrified by that fact and that the father of her baby had run like a rabbit from parenthood, so she was facing it all alone. But that *was* the second time he'd said he pitied her....

"He feels sorry for me?"

Hutch Kincaid chuckled. "He thinks you're *pretty.*"

The dizziness finally passed and Issa could see straight again. She cast a glance at the little boy who, despite his undefined features, resembled the man too much not to be closely related to him, and said an uncertain, "Thank you?"

"Wilcome."

"That's *you're welcome,*" her landlord translated. "And this is Asher, by the way. My son. He's two and a half, with a mind of his own. And he's apparently developing a taste in women..." Hutch Kincaid added somewhat under his breath, sounding amused.

Issa got to her feet then and was rewarded with a closer view of her hubba-hubba-handsome landlord.

And oh, but he *was* hubba-hubba-handsome, more so now that he was smiling slightly, a smile that drew lines from the corners of his nose to bracket his nimble-looking mouth.

But she was in absolutely no position to be paying any attention whatsoever to how handsome he was, she reminded herself.

"I'm sorry, I don't usually sleep in the daytime, but I was really out of it..." she lied. The truth was that lately sleeping was all she wanted to do night *and* day, and napping had become nothing unusual for her.

"It's okay," Hutch Kincaid assured her in an understanding tone, his gaze dropping for a split second to the pamphlets, making it clear that he'd seen them and put two and two together.

And that was when something else occurred to Issa.

While she hadn't met Hutch Kincaid before this, she'd learned through her brother and half sister that he was connected to her family through his own family and friends.

And this was Northbridge where word could travel like wildfire....

All of which made her think she'd better address the subject right away.

"Yes, I'm pregnant. And unmarried, unattached—" Why was she telling him *that?*

Oh, she was just never, *ever* at her best meeting new people. She always made blunders, and now, when she was already thrown off-kilter by her overall situation, when it was all too fresh for her to have become comfortable with, she supposed she shouldn't be shocked that she was particularly bumbling.

She shook her head as if that would erase her awkwardness and tried to make enough sense of what she was saying to get her point across. "No one here—*no one*—knows, so *please*—"

Hutch Kincaid held up one hand, palm out. "It's okay. It won't come from me," he said.

But still feeling exposed, Issa scooped up the pamphlets and shoved them under the couch cushion to get them out of sight.

Then, desperate to regain some sense of normalcy, she said, "Can I have just a minute to splash some water on my face? Maybe you could look at the lock while I do..."

"Sure," the big man agreed.

And Issa made a beeline to the bathroom.

For a moment after she reached it, she merely leaned her back against the door she'd shut firmly behind herself. Closing her eyes, she dropped her head forward and again shook it—this time cursing the shyness that she'd always suffered, that had once again made her act like a ninny. Why couldn't she just be smooth?

But it was too late for that with her landlord. He probably already thought she was an idiot. An unmarried, pregnant idiot.

Nothing like making a good first impression....

Oh, no, and she hadn't even introduced herself! He'd introduced *himself.* And his son. But she'd overlooked that simple civility, too.

I really am a ninny. A socially inept ninny....

Disgusted with herself, Issa sighed and pushed away from the door. To her right was the sink, to her left was the linen closet that was hidden when the bathroom door was open.

She turned and rummaged in the linen closet.

The apartment was small—a single bedroom, a

single bath, with the living room, kitchen and dining area all in the one open space she'd just fled. She liked the place, though. She'd been told that the remodel that had turned it into a duplex had only recently been completed, and that everything was new, including all the furnishings. She'd needed only her own towels, linens and kitchenware, so unpacking had been easily accomplished in the two days she'd been living there.

She took a washcloth and a hand towel from the closet and rotated to face the sink.

Wetting the washcloth, she buried her face in it and hoped for a surge of the energy and oomph that pregnancy seemed to have robbed her of. But still she just wanted to sleep.

Maybe it was some kind of psychological need to escape the situation she'd found herself in.

Except that the pamphlets said to expect to feel fatigued and to need some extra rest as her body adjusted.

Hurry up and adjust, she told herself. Because she had a whole lot more to deal with than mere hormones.

She dried her face and took a look in the mirror above the sink.

Rosy glow—the pamphlets had talked about that, too, and surprisingly, Issa could see it. She'd always had an extremely pale complexion, but now her coloring couldn't be better—her high cheekbones were petal pink, making her look robustly healthy even without blush.

That was a good thing, she thought. One of the few advantages to pregnancy.

That and the fact that her previously A-cup breasts had already gone to a B. She didn't have any complaints about that, either.

And in spite of how tired she felt most of the time, there weren't any circles under her blue-green eyes— she was grateful for that. At least nothing gave away how she felt.

Now if only the pamphlets were wrong about the potential for hair loss or dullness. She liked her light, flaxen hair the way it was—although at the moment one side of it had escaped the clip that had been holding the shoulder-length locks at the back of her head and it looked awful.

Great, bedhead...

Another way in which she was not happy to have met Hutch Kincaid.

She took the clip out, quickly ran a brush through her hair and then caught it in the back again where she reclipped it.

Sprucing up for her handsome landlord?

That wasn't what she was doing, she reasoned. She just wanted to be presentable.

Which was also why she applied the light lip gloss.

And when it came to adding a touch of mascara even though she hadn't put any on earlier today? That was just so she looked more bright-eyed and not like some slug-a-bed who slept the afternoons away.

In her clothes....

How did they look?

Checking, she judged that her jeans showed no evidence that she'd been sleeping in them. She just wished that they weren't her puttering-around-the-house jeans, that they were her better jeans. One of the other pairs that didn't sag in the seat.

Not that it mattered what her seat did.

As for the cap-sleeved T-shirt she had on? It was

slightly rumpled, so she tugged on the hem to stretch the wrinkles out of it. That pulled the V-neckline lower, although not low enough to show cleavage. But because the T-shirt was a bit on the snug side, it still showed off the single visible clue that she was pregnant—her blossoming chest.

Why that had even crossed her mind she didn't know. It shouldn't have.

But the new B-cups did make her T-shirts look a lot better. It was just about her general appearance, and had nothing whatsoever to do with who might see her. It was a confidence builder. And she definitely needed that!

Okay, presentable—she just wanted to be presentable and she was.

So get back out there to the landlord...

She took a deep breath, exhaled it completely and told herself to try to have some composure, to be more outgoing than she was naturally inclined to be. The shyness had never served her well and it certainly wasn't helping now.

Another deep breath and she opened the bathroom door.

When she did, she could see Hutch Kincaid in the vicinity of the apartment's entrance again, this time with his back to her as he fiddled with the door handle.

The rear view of him was no less impressive than the front. *His* jeans definitely didn't sag in the seat. Instead, he sported a derriere to die for, splendidly displayed in denim.

And from there up? Her gaze began at his narrow waist and rose to broad, broad shoulders that didn't have the slightest hunch to them. Nope, straight and strong-looking, they formed a V-shaped canvas that squared into biceps straining the short sleeves of his polo shirt with well-defined muscles.

Okay, so there was nothing lacking in the man's physique. It still didn't matter to her.

"I just realized that I didn't introduce myself," she said when he changed angles and caught sight of her coming out of the bathroom. "I'm sure you know, but I'm Issa McKendrick. I didn't mean to be rude."

"Itta?" the little boy said from where he was hunkered down near the door, playing with a screwdriver and a pair of pliers.

"Issa," she corrected.

"Itta," the toddler countered as if he'd said it right the first time.

"That's probably as good as it's gonna get," Hutch Kincaid said as he put the screwdriver he'd been using in one of the back pockets of his jeans. Then he put one hand on the knob on the outside of the door and the other on the inside knob. Cupping them, he slowly turned them both back and forth, back and forth...

And out of nowhere Issa suddenly had a flash of something far less innocent being done with those hands. And her own new B-cups.

Where *that* had come from she had no idea and she was so stunned by it that for a moment she didn't know what to do.

Then she realized her landlord had no idea what had just shot through her mind and that she needed to ignore it herself. So, still not wanting to be a shrinking violet, Issa attempted to make small talk while he worked.

"I've known your brother Chase since I was a kid—

he was at our house so much growing up that he was like one of us."

"I've heard that. He's talked about how unhappy he was with his foster father. We all hate that he didn't get adopted the way the rest of us did."

"It came as such a surprise to find out that he had biological brothers and sisters."

"It came as a surprise to us, too," Hutch said.

Hutch's birth parents had been killed in a car accident when Hutch and his twin brother, Ian, were two months old, leaving behind five children—Hutch, Ian, an older sister named Shannon, their older brother, Chase, and a much older half sister, Angie. Angie had been returned to her birth father, the three youngest children had been adopted to two different homes, while Chase had been placed in foster care and grown up in Northbridge, best friends with Issa's half brother Logan.

It was Angie who remembered the other four siblings, who sought them out and revealed that there were brothers and another sister when she'd faced the end of her own life and needed someone to raise her son.

"All that time Chase had all these brothers and sisters he didn't know about..." Issa marveled.

"And now there's also our half sister Angie's son, Cody, to round things out," Hutch added.

"Right. A nephew Chase is *raising*—it's hard to picture the Chase I knew as a dad. But the whole thing was just amazing. I was here at Christmastime, so I met Shannon and Cody then, and I heard before I left that they'd contacted you and your twin—"

"Ian," he supplied.

"Right. I've only been in town a couple of days, so I

haven't met him yet, but I knew that was his name. Ian Kincaid. And you're Hutch..."

And she was babbling.

She was just no good at this.

Plus it didn't help that it had suddenly occurred to her that Hutch Kincaid had exactly the same color eyes as his older brother, Chase. And that she'd always thought that Chase's eyes were gorgeous....

Hutch Kincaid made it easier on her then by picking up the conversation and running with it.

"And we're even in-laws now."

It was true. Hutch's newly found sister Shannon had recently married Issa's brother Dag, although Issa had not been able to attend the ceremony. Her plane had been grounded due to weather.

"I came to Northbridge for Shannon's wedding," Hutch continued. "That was my first trip here since Ian and I were adopted and taken to Billings. The wedding was at the end of March. Through April and May I've been here off and on, so I'm only beginning to get to know who's who. Logan and Dag I've seen a lot of, and I've heard there's more to your family but I haven't met the others."

"And you and Ash live downstairs..."

"For now. I bought the place as an investment. It was a flip—I guess it was pretty run-down when the owners put it on the market, but the local contractor bought it, remodeled it and put it up for resale. I figured I could rent both halves out to college kids in the fall, and in the meantime Ash and I needed somewhere to stay while I look for a house for the two of us. Dag said you needed pretty much the same thing—somewhere to stay short-term—"

"While I look for a house to buy, too."

"So you're settling back in your old hometown?"

"I am," she said without going into any details, even though she was relieved that he was making conversation and facilitating an easy flow between them.

"Northbridge has plenty of charm," Hutch said. "It sucked me in at first glance and I haven't found anything about it that I don't like yet. I even bought out the old sporting goods store to turn into one of mine."

Beyond his connection to Chase, her half brother Logan's best friend and business partner, Issa really only knew two things about Hutch Kincaid.

She knew that he and his twin had been raised by former football giant and three-time Super Bowl-winning quarterback Morgan Kincaid. *The* Morgan Kincaid, who had parlayed his football fame and fortune into the Kincaid Corporation—a conglomerate of retail, rental and hotel properties, car dealerships, restaurants and various other ventures that now included his most recent purchase, an NFL expansion team that he was bringing to Montana—the Monarchs. Their training center was to be built in Northbridge.

The other thing she knew about Hutch Kincaid—only because Dag had told her—was that he'd had his own star-quality career in football at some point but now owned sporting goods stores.

"What's it called, your store?"

"Stores, plural. The one here will be my fifth. They're Kincaid's All Sports. There's a website, too. We do a respectable share of online business."

"Cool…"

Cool? Had she really just said that? Issa wanted to kick herself.

Trying to get past the awkwardness as fast as she could, she angled her gaze down to Hutch Kincaid's son. "What about you, Asher? Do you like sports?" she asked, fearing that sounded almost as dumb as *cool.*

"I yice cookies..." the toddler answered with an obvious hint.

"I don't have any cookies," Issa whispered to Hutch.

"No, no, no," Hutch Kincaid said with another chuckle. "You don't *need* to have cookies. Two-and-a-half-year-olds aren't known for their manners." Then to his son, he said, "No cookies, Ash."

Hutch stopped fiddling with the lock and straightened up to face Issa. "I'm gonna have to cry uncle with this lock anyway—it can't be fixed. I'll have to get a new one and come back. Is that okay?"

Somehow the thought that she was going to see him again was energizing. And Issa had no idea why that was the case. Why adrenaline instantly flooded her to chase away her pregnancy-induced weariness.

What she did know was that excitement over a second visit was not a response she should be having....

"Would you mind if it was this evening, though?" he was saying into her confused thoughts. "I'll hit the hardware store, but there are some things I needed to check on at my new store and it's just a few doors down, so I'd like to kill two birds with one stone. Then Ash will need some dinner. Can we make it after that?"

"Sure," Issa said, wondering if her voice had sounded as bright and full of anticipation to him as it had to her. She hoped not. Then, working for a more neutral tone, she added, "I'll be here."

Had she sounded unduly eager and available? Or worse yet, a little desperate?

She wasn't. She wasn't at all desperate. Not for company. Not for a man. Not for anything. Except for that composure she'd been hoping to find when she'd come out of the bathroom.

But then she started to think of Hutch Kincaid being in town in the early June heat, meeting people on the street, in the hardware store. Talking to them. She thought of the chance that he might tell her secret. And composure slipped further out of her reach.

"You won't forget not to say anything to anyone, though, right?"

Having given up trying to fix the door handle, he'd removed it along with the built-in lock and was gathering up the pieces when she said that. He cast her a confused look that told her he didn't know what she was referring to.

"About… You know… Earlier… The pamphlets…" She just couldn't bring herself to say it outright again.

"Oh, yeah," he said when what she was talking about finally seemed to dawn on him. Then he smiled slightly and added, "See, forgotten already. No, I won't say a thing to anyone. It's your business."

"And maybe I'll have cookies when you get back," she said too jovially, overcompensating and once more proving how clumsy she could be.

"I yice cookies," Ash Kincaid contributed.

"Don't go out of your way—you don't have to do that," her landlord assured her.

"Well, we'll see," Issa said.

Hutch Kincaid glanced down at his son then. "Come on, buddy, time to go. Give me the pliers and screwdriver."

The little boy stood from his squat on the floor.

Rather than handing his father the tools, he pulled up his striped T-shirt—exposing his entire tummy—twisted as far around as he could and put them into the back pockets of his own jeans, obviously mimicking his father.

But Hutch Kincaid reached down and took them out again. "We don't need you falling back on those," he explained as he did.

Then he tugged the toddler's shirt down, and held out one long index finger. Without prompting, the toddler took it in one chubby fist.

"Say goodbye to Issa," Hutch instructed.

"'Bye, Itta."

"'Bye, Ash," Issa answered.

"We'll be back around seven," Hutch Kincaid said.

"Okay."

"And your secret is safe with me, so don't worry about it," he said in a softer voice.

Issa looked squarely at him, searching for signs of disapproval or judgment. But there seemed to be only kindness and understanding in his remarkable blue eyes.

"Thanks," she said, not only sounding relieved but actually feeling it.

He nodded at the hole in the door where the handle and lock had been. "You can still close the door. It won't be any worse than it was with the bad hardware. I'll lock the main door downstairs and we'll be gone, so you'll have the place to yourself until I come back with the new stuff—no more surprise visitors."

"Sure. Okay," Issa muttered as he took his son and left her to do as he'd suggested, shutting her door as securely as she could.

And then she found herself doing the oddest thing.

She bent over and peeked through the hole where the handle had been to watch her landlord go down the stairs that led to his own half of the house.

At least until she realized what she was doing and how silly it was.

Then she shot upright and reminded herself that no matter how big and strapping and hubba-hubba-handsome someone was, so much as noticing a man at this point was beyond absurd. She was pregnant. With another man's baby. And that was more than enough of a catastrophe. She didn't need to add insult to injury.

But Hutch Kincaid *was* big, strapping and hubba-hubba-handsome.

And nice, too, it seemed.

It just didn't change anything.

Chapter Two

"One more bite, Ash, then we'll go upstairs and fix Issa's door."

"Itta," Ash parroted his father before dragging a French fry through a puddle of ketchup and putting it haphazardly into his mouth. Then, mid-chew, the two-and-a-half-year-old announced for the third time, "Done."

The toddler had eaten about half of his dinner and Hutch had been urging him to eat more for at least fifteen minutes. One bite at a time. He decided to finally accept the *done* decree. What he wasn't sure of was whether Ash was too young yet for etiquette lessons, but he decided to err on the side of caution and said, "Don't talk with your mouth full, big guy."

"'Kay," Ash agreed, giving Hutch his second view of the partially chewed fry.

So much for that.

Hutch got up from the table, slid Ash's sippy cup to the little boy and said, "Finish your milk," as he gathered the remnants of their burgers and fries to put into the trash.

Teaching table manners—Iris would approve of that even if he had failed at it.

Burgers and fries for Sunday dinner—his late wife would have frowned on that.

Still, it was a meal, they'd sat at the kitchen table together to eat it and Hutch had attempted to give the etiquette lesson—that was all something. Something better than the way things had been right after Iris had died. Because while he might not be a candidate for Father of the Year, he *was* giving Ash his all now.

And in that vein, he made a mental note to look in the child-development books for information on when and how to begin teaching table manners, and when to reasonably expect a kid to understand and be able to incorporate them into his routine.

As for the fast food that he tried to keep to a minimum, they *had* just arrived home from a seven-day trip to Denver where Hutch had closed on the sale of his and Iris's house. Plus he'd come home to details that needed to be attended to with the new store, and an upstairs tenant who had arrived during his absence and needed him to take care of the broken lock on the apartment door—sometimes fast food was just a necessity.

As it was, he was still five minutes late for getting upstairs to the apartment.

He glanced over his shoulder as he did the dishes. Ash's sippy cup was right where he'd left it.

"Finish your milk, Ash," he repeated. "It'll make you big and strong."

"Lise you," Ash said.

"Yep, like me," Hutch confirmed, feeling that twinge of delight that his son's current hero worship gave him. The books said things like that came and went with the different stages kids passed through, but Hutch was enjoying it while it lasted. "Let's see your muscles."

Ash raised his arms in flexing He-Man fashion, fists pointed toward his tiny shoulders.

"They're lookin' good, but I think they need some more milk. Drink up."

The tiny tot took the sippy cup and finally drank from it.

Hutch wasn't sure whether encouragement along those lines translated into the kind of pressure his own father had put on him and Ian to be athletes—actually, to be football stars to equal Morgan Kincaid's own accomplishments as a former NFL player. Hutch hoped not. Pressuring Ash was definitely not something he wanted to do. The be-like-Dad, muscle-building angle just seemed to be one that worked, so Hutch was using it. He'd stop if it ever started to become anything more than a ploy.

He just wanted to be a good dad. He wanted to incorporate the parts of his own father that he'd liked and appreciated, and leave out the parts that hadn't been great. And he wanted to do the kind of job his late wife would have expected of him, the kind of job Iris would be counting on him to do.

"Yook now," Ash demanded.

Hutch glanced over his shoulder once more. The sippy cup was drained and Ash was again flexing.

"Yep, I can see those muscles growing already. Good job!"

Dishes finally in the dishwasher, Hutch rinsed the sink, then dampened a paper towel and returned to the kitchen table where Ash sat in a booster seat propped on one of the chairs.

"Cleanup," he announced.

"No!" Ash protested the way he always did when it came to washing his face.

"Come on, Issa is expecting us and we can't visit a lady with ketchup all over your face and hands."

"Itta's pit-tee," Ash said, seeming more inclined toward cooperation with the mention of Issa.

"Yes, she is," Hutch confirmed as he applied the damp cloth to the toddler.

Thoughts of Issa, images of her, hadn't been far from Hutch's mind since he'd first set eyes on her this afternoon. Mentioning her name to his son, Ash's comment about her, were all it took to bring her to the forefront yet again.

Sleeping Beauty, that had been Hutch's first impression.

The incredible beauty sleeping on the couch in the apartment upstairs.

When her brother Dag had rented the apartment for her, he'd told Hutch that his sister was quiet and the shiest of all the McKendricks. That she was meticulous and tidy so she would be a good tenant. Dag hadn't said anything about the fact that Issa was a head turner.

Not that that was at all relevant to renting her a temporary place to live.

It was just that, to Hutch, Issa McKendrick was something to behold and he sort of wished he'd known that in advance so he hadn't been so dumbstruck at first.

She was a vision that made him not quite believe his own eyes.

Flaxen hair and skin like porcelain—those had been the first two things to strike him.

And she had the most delicate features—a straight, unmarred forehead; a gently sloping nose; a slightly rounded chin; full, petal pink lips; rosy, high cheekbones; and when she'd smiled slightly in her sleep, there had been dimples. Deep, deep dimples in both cheeks.

And then she'd opened her eyes. And even from across the room he'd been able to see how blue they were. Dark, sapphire blue—they stood out strikingly amidst that light skin and hair. Sparkling dark sapphires...

She was breathtakingly beautiful but still with a wholesomeness to her.

But stunning or not, it didn't make any difference.

Hutch was not in the market for a woman. Sure, a year and a half of widowerhood might mean that he could be. But he wasn't. He had Ash to think of. To focus on. He had to concentrate on being a single father. A father to his own kid. This was no time to get into anything with any woman, let alone with someone who had issues of her own to deal with—issues like a baby on the way without a dad.

But Issa McKendrick wasn't going to be hard to look at while they both lived here, he thought as he lifted his son down from the booster seat.

He just wasn't interested in anything more than looking. The way he might look at a painting or a sculpture or a photograph—purely as an appreciation for a thing of beauty. A woman of beauty.

But there was no doubt about it, Issa McKendrick was definitely that.

* * *

"Itta hep. I'ma eat cookies."

"I think I've been had," Issa observed.

Hutch Kincaid laughed. "I think you have."

In anticipation of Hutch and his son coming to install her new door handle and lock, Issa had run to the store and bought cookies for the little boy. She'd set some of them out on a plate on the coffee table.

Hutch had made a great show of Ash being his assistant, enlisting his son to hand him the screwdriver when he asked for it.

"Then when you're finished," Issa had said, "there are cookies…"

That had drawn Ash's attention to the dish on the coffee table. But a mere glance in that direction was the tot's only immediate response.

What he had done was lure Issa into helping Hutch, too, handing the screwdriver to her so that she could hand it to Hutch.

Issa had thought it was cute that the toddler wanted to include her. And in an attempt to be more outgoing and friendly, she'd complied.

But once Ash had her at the door with Hutch, holding the screwdriver, the little boy made the announcement that she could play assistant while he went to have a cookie.

"How can a two-and-a-half-year-old be that tricky?" she asked.

"Hey, when cookies are involved, it's every man for himself," Hutch said with a laugh before he called after his son, "One, Ash. You can have one cookie."

Then turning back to Issa, Hutch whispered, "Now watch, he's going to take a bite out of one, say he doesn't like it, choose another, take a bite, and do the same thing until he's had a taste of every kind you have out there."

"I shouldn't have bought the assortment?"

"You can't put that much temptation in front of him."

"I don't know anything about raising kids," Issa confessed.

But apparently Hutch Kincaid did because Ash had done exactly what his father had predicted and was on to his second cookie.

"One, Ash," Hutch warned.

"I doan yice this kind," the toddler announced for the second time, choosing a third cookie.

"Better take the plate away," Hutch advised Issa.

"It's okay. I put them out for him. And there are only four kinds. Technically, if he has one bite of each kind, it'll add up to only one cookie."

"Great, you want to split hairs, too. The problem with that logic is that there are more than four cookies on that plate and he'll go on taking one bite out of every cookie unless he's stopped. Can you hold this like this?"

That last question drew Issa's gaze from son back to father.

Hutch had been working at lining up the inside doorknob with the outside doorknob and—the same way he had earlier in the day when he'd inspired inappropriate ideas in her—he had a hand on each of them.

"If you don't keep them where I've got them I'll have to line them up all over again," he explained when she was slow in responding to his question.

"Oh, sure," she said, stepping to his side to replace

him before her imagination went any further than it already had.

And if, in the transfer, his hands brushed hers and set off tiny sparks? She wrote that off to static electricity, even though that wasn't what it had been.

Maintaining the position of the door handles, she looked on as Hutch crossed to the coffee table and picked up the plate as well as the cookies his son had discarded.

"No!" Ash rebelled.

"You can have *one,*" Hutch reminded reasonably, firmly, without any anger or aggravation.

"I wanna diff'ent one."

"Nope, the one in your hand will have to do," Hutch informed him, setting the plate on the top shelf of the nearby bookcase and stacking the already-bitten cookies beside it.

Ash studied the situation intently.

Issa couldn't be sure, but she had the impression that the toddler was working on a plan to climb up to that plate.

But Hutch again seemed to read his son's mind. "Don't even try it," he warned as he headed for the door again. "Just eat your cookie."

Ash scowled at his father but proceeded to taste his final selection.

Issa couldn't help laughing a little at it all as Hutch returned to the door, smiling as if he understood her amusement.

"Can you keep hanging on while I screw them in?" he said when he got to her.

"Sure," she said a second time, at a loss for why so

much about this man and even perfectly innocent things he said seemed suggestive to her.

Maybe it was hormones.

Or maybe she'd spent too much time teaching teenagers who could rarely think or talk about anything else.

One way or another, she really needed to curb it, she told herself.

There was silence for the first few minutes of their joint endeavor and during that time Issa couldn't help looking at Hutch.

She was glad she hadn't indulged her inclination to change clothes for tonight, that the only thing she'd done was brush her hair out and leave it down. She'd told herself that it would be too obvious if she put on a different outfit, that it would give away the fact that she'd been singularly—and strangely—focused on when she was going to get to be with him again. And now that she could see that he hadn't been inclined to change his clothes for her, she thought it was a good thing she hadn't changed hers for him.

Not that he didn't look just as stare-worthy tonight as he had earlier, because he did. And she was never more aware of that fact than when he had leaned over to pick up those cookies.

But she'd lectured herself about not paying any attention to things like that and so she was trying not to.

Of course, it might help to do something besides ogling him while he worked close enough for her to catch the scent of a cologne that smelled like a cool, clear summer day at the beach. She just couldn't think of anything to say to distract herself.

Then, as Hutch began to apply screwdriver to the

second screw to fasten the inside and outside knobs together, he offered her that distraction by making conversation.

"Issa—that's not an ordinary name," he said then.

"It's short for Isadora."

"Still not ordinary. And there's Dag, and some others I've heard..."

"There's my sister Tessa—Tessa is short for Theodora. And my sister Zeli, but she's just Zeli. Our mother thought our names sounded European and that anything European was sophisticated. And unfortunately she was all about putting on airs. But it isn't as if Hutch is a common name. Or Ash, either," Issa pointed out.

"Hutch is short for Hutchenson. It was on the birth certificate and because my birth parents weren't around to explain it, I can't tell you where it came from. I can tell you that Asher was a family name on Ash's mom's side—her grandfather."

"I see," Issa said, panicking slightly because he'd initiated this subject and she couldn't think of what to come back with now that it seemed to be her turn.

But again Hutch Kincaid made it easy on her by not expecting her to take a turn. "So you're a teacher, I think Dag said..."

"High school freshman chemistry. Or at least I *was* a teacher. In Seattle. But a little more than a year ago I sort of accidentally invented something and that allowed me to... Oh, it's complicated," she concluded when she was afraid she might bore him.

"What did you invent?" he asked, not letting her off the hook so easily.

"Well, in its toy version, it's called Gob-o-Goo—"

"I've seen that at the toy store! It's sort of like putty?"

"Right, except that it doesn't ever dry out, it will hold whatever shape it's put into, but then can be remolded whenever anyone wants to. Plus it's not harmful if kids eat it—not that it's food, but it just won't hurt anything if kids put it in their mouth."

"And you *accidentally* invented it?"

"It really was an accident. I was working at home on an experiment for the Reactions in the Kitchen lesson, trying to jazz it up a little to make it more exciting—it isn't easy to keep ninth graders' interest—" Because they were so often thinking about whoever was in front of them the way she was thinking about Hutch at that moment, about the way his hair curled just the slightest bit at his nape...

Issa again reined in her wandering thoughts to continue what she was saying.

"Anyway, I reached for something, knocked a whole box of baking soda into what I already had in the bowl—"

"And ta-da?"

"Pretty much. After the mixture went kind of crazy, it stabilized and *then* ta-da. It looked like a soft, shiny cloud and I just couldn't seem to resist touching it to see how it felt."

Much the way she wanted to touch his hair and see how it felt....

Luckily her hands were occupied with doorknobs.

"It felt as good as it looked and it was fun to mess with." The way she *couldn't* mess with her landlord, she warned herself. "Long story short, it took some tweaking from there, but I kept going back to it, fiddling with it, and Gob-o-Goo was born. A friend worked for a toy company and she helped me patent it and sell it to them."

"That's not a story you hear every day," he said.

"It really was just a fluke, though. I almost feel weird taking credit for it."

"And what did you mean when you said *in its toy version?*" Hutch asked then.

He really paid attention…

"That was kind of a fluke, too. One day I was messing around with it when the phone rang. I sort of unconsciously kept squeezing it and squishing it while I talked. Then I had the idea of turning it into something therapeutic. A distant, aging relative years ago broke her arm and I remembered her squeezing a ball as part of her physical therapy to increase the strength in that hand when she was recovering. At first she was too weak to do it and I started to think that my stuff had just enough resistance that it might work better than the ball in the first stages of rehab therapy."

Okay, now she was thinking about squeezing the biceps her gaze had somehow attached itself to. What was wrong with her?

Averting her eyes, she said, "Anyway—again—" Because she knew she'd already said *anyway* once before. "I went back to the patent attorney, told him my idea and second ta-da. It's being used as a filler substance to manufacture a new therapeutic tool."

"That's impressive," Hutch said.

"Not really. Not when you know that it was honestly all unintentional. Accidental."

"Still, those are more fortunate accidents than I've ever had."

"They did allow me to quit working for the time being so I could move back to Northbridge. That was the biggest benefit because I was at loose ends in Seattle and staying there would have been... I just didn't want to do it," she finished, deciding belatedly that she didn't want to get into the subject of the bad turn of romantic events that had driven her home.

So she skirted that issue. "And I'll be able to buy a house without having to worry about money for a while. So yeah, that all does make it a fortunate accident," she conceded. "But I can't pretend that Gob-o-Goo or the squishy ball were born from the grand design of some sort of brainiac, either, because they really just came from my being a klutz."

"I think you're being modest."

"I'm really not," she insisted.

And how had her eyes gotten back on him again? This time on his profile? His perfect profile...

"Okay, you can let go."

She heard the words as if from a distance. But the message didn't immediately sink in because she was adrift in studying the side view of his face.

Then, from right next to her, Ash echoed his father with a "Y'et go."

Issa hadn't been aware of the toddler rejoining them after apparently having given up trying to figure out a way to get to that plate of cookies. But his voice brought her to her senses. She took her hands from the door handles and stepped back as Hutch Kincaid tested them.

Moving farther into the room, she hoped distance might help cure the weird affliction she seemed to have when it came to this man. But even that didn't keep her from being overly **aware of** every little detail as he closed the door to make **sure** it actually stayed closed. He did a few trial runs **with the** keys—with the door open and finally with it closed, ultimately locking himself out and then letting himself in again.

"Looks like we're in business! Now you can lock your door and keep your nosy neighbors out."

Too bad she couldn't keep the unwelcome thoughts she kept having about him out of her head....

He had two sets of keys and he held one set out to her then. "Keys for you, keys for me just in case of emergency—but *only* if there's an emergency or you lock yourself out or something."

Issa held out her palm. Then she tried not to think about the fact that the keys were warm from his hand.

"I wan some," Ash complained.

Hutch dug into his pocket and produced an entire ring full of keys. "Here you go, big guy, you can hang on to these, but don't lose them."

Ash accepted the keys and jammed them into his own jean pocket. And again Issa was reasonably certain that the child was mimicking what he'd seen his father do innumerable times.

"'Nother cookie?" Ash suggested hopefully then.

"Nope, you and I are gonna leave Issa alone and go downstairs so you can have your bath and get ready for bed."

"No bath, no bed!" Ash protested once more.

"Yes bath, yes bed," Hutch Kincaid countered, reaching out to palm his son's buzz-cut, sandy-colored head like a basketball.

"I doan wanna," the toddler grumbled.

"How about if I let you take one more cookie home

with you and after your bath, you can have it with your milk while I read your Thomas the Train book?" Then as an afterthought, Hutch said, "If Issa is willing to let you have another cookie."

"Sure," she said for the third time. "He can take the whole—"

"Shh," Hutch cut her short, holding a long index finger to his lips to stop her before she went on.

"I wan chock-it," Ash announced by way of conceding to the deal.

"Chocolate it is," Issa said, going to the dish on the bookshelf and choosing the chocolate sandwich cookie with the white cream center.

As she gave it to Ash, his father said, "What do you say?"

"S'ank you."

"You're welcome," Issa responded.

"Okay, why don't you go downstairs and put your cookie in the kitchen, and I'll be right there. Remember how much you like to dunk it, so if you eat it before you get your milk, you'll miss that," Hutch said then, opening the door to let his son out.

"'Bye, Itta," Ash said without prompting.

"'Bye, Ash," Issa answered, wondering why Hutch Kincaid was hanging back.

His son had just begun the slow descent down the stairs when Hutch turned his attention to Issa again to say, "The dinner tomorrow night at Meg and Logan's? I talked to Shannon late this afternoon and she said you're going, too. She pointed out that we might as well go together? That it's silly to take two cars?"

Issa hadn't really thought about Hutch Kincaid going to dinner at her half brother's house Monday night, but now that he said it, it made sense that he was. It was a barbecue at the Mackey and McKendrick compound that would include Hutch's brother Chase, nephew, Cody, and Chase's wife, Hadley, who was Issa's half sister. Hutch's twin, Ian, and Ian's fiancée, Jenna, would also be there. Plus Hutch's sister Shannon and Issa's brother Dag were also going.

Hutch's invitation to share a ride, though, was worded a little oddly—it was Shannon's idea and Hutch had delivered it as if he wasn't completely sold on it.

Maybe he didn't want them to go together.

"It doesn't matter. If you hadn't planned to go from here, if you were going straight from your store or something, I can get there on my own."

"No, I actually planned to bring Ash home for a late nap so he'll be rested before we go—he's more likely to behave that way—so I'll be leaving from here. But it's up to you. I don't want you to feel like you *have* to go anywhere with me because we live here the way we do. But it does make sense to carpool…."

Still not an enthusiastic sales pitch.

"Are you sure you want me?" Oh, that hadn't come out right. "To ride along," she added as if that would make it better.

But it was already too late because there was a hint of a smile on Hutch Kincaid's lips. Then, as if he'd decided to confess something, he said, "Dag told me you were kind of shy, that you aren't comfortable around most people until you really get to know them. I just don't want to push you and have you do something you don't want to do."

Damn Dag. He was still her little brother giving away things about her that she didn't want out in the open—like when he'd announced her shoe size at church one Sunday.

"It's okay," Issa felt as if she had to say. "We've kind of gotten to know each other today—I know you're an ex-football player turned sporting goods store owner, you know I'm a ninth-grade chemistry teacher and accidental inventor...."

Hutch Kincaid's slight smile went full-on. "We're practically old friends," he said facetiously. "Does that mean we can drive over together?"

At that moment Issa didn't know what they would talk about again and that made her nervous. But so far he *hadn't* been difficult to be with because he was good at making conversation himself. And riding to the dinner with him tomorrow night *would* give her the opportunity to remind him not to spill the beans about her pregnancy....

"I think we could probably drive over together," she decreed. "But you don't have to drive. I mean, I can drive. We can take my car if you want." She was nervous and cut herself off before it went too far.

"I don't suppose you've had any experience with the car seat issue yet," he said like an old sage. "It's easiest to take whatever vehicle it's already strapped into."

"Does that leave room for me?"

"Plenty. I have a fairly big SUV and car seats have to be in the back. You can have my passenger seat all to yourself."

"Okay, then. I guess if it's all right with you, it's all right with me."

"We'll be doing our small part to save the environment," he concluded. "Tomorrow night, shortly before six?"

"Sure." Couldn't she say anything else? That was four times! She hoped he wasn't counting. "I can meet you downstairs."

"I'll see you there and then."

"There and then," Issa echoed, wishing after the fact that she hadn't.

That was when Hutch Kincaid should have left, but he didn't. He stayed where he was, standing in her doorway, staring at her, studying her.

"Okay, then," he muttered after a moment, as if his mind was somewhere else. "And if the lock gives you any trouble, you know where to find me."

Somehow that had sounded a bit awkward on his part, although Issa couldn't imagine why Hutch Kincaid would feel at all ill at ease saying goodbye to her.

"I do know where to find you," she confirmed.

"Anything else you need, too."

"Thanks."

He really was having trouble leaving. She didn't know why, but it made her want to smile.

Then he seemed to jolt out of his reverie. "Okay, see you tomorrow."

"See you tomorrow."

But another split second still went by before Hutch Kincaid followed his son out her door and, without another glance in Issa's direction, went down the stairs.

And yet just the fact that he seemed to have been even a touch gawky at the end made her feel so much better.

It even made it easier for her to think about riding over to her half brother's place with him the next night.

Which she suddenly found herself looking forward to.

Chapter Three

"Oh. Wine."

"Not just *any* wine, Issa, this is from that little vineyard in Napa that you like so much," Logan said when Issa hesitated to accept his offer of a glass of wine. She, Hutch and Ash had just arrived at the Mackey and McKendrick compound for Monday evening's barbecue.

It hadn't occurred to her that not being able to drink because of her pregnancy would raise questions. Ordinarily she would have gratefully accepted the glass of wine and enjoyed it and the relaxing benefits that would have helped her be more comfortable socializing. That was something that her half and whole siblings Logan, Hadley and Dag knew well. Which was likely why Logan had gone out of his way to get her favorite wine. And why it looked all the more suspicious that she was holding back.

But she couldn't drink. And she also couldn't think fast enough to come up with a plausible excuse.

Maybe she should say yes to the wine, have one tiny sip for show, then pour the rest of it out by small increments when no one seemed to be looking, and hope she didn't get caught.

"Oops, she promised to be my designated driver tonight, so I started early and had a beer before we left," Hutch jumped in suddenly, saving the day.

"I saw your SUV out front, Hutch. You came in that instead of Issa's car even though she's driving?" Hadley asked.

Luckily no one had seen them actually pull up or they would have known that Hutch had driven.

"Car seat!" Issa said, her brain finally functioning so she could help things along. "It was more trouble to switch it to my car, so I just said I'd drive Hutch's. But now that I'm committed, no wine for me. I appreciate that you went to the trouble, though."

"We'll open it another time," Meg interjected, moving things along. "How about iced tea or lemonade? And Hutch, you're drinking beer?"

"Tall and cold!" Hutch said with vigor, making everyone laugh and drawing the focus off Issa.

To Issa's relief.

"I can pour my own lemonade," Issa said, grabbing the pitcher from the kitchen table.

"Then, because we're all here, we can take everything out back," Meg suggested.

In the backyard Chase was manning a big barbecue grill. Standing nearby overseeing things were the rest of the guests—Shannon, Dag, Jenna Bowen—whom Issa knew because they'd both grown up in the small town, and another man who had to be Hutch Kincaid's twin because they looked so much alike that Issa could have picked him out of a crowd.

The barbecue contingent greeted Issa and Hutch as they came out onto the back porch carrying whatever they could manage of beverages and condiments—the last of what was needed to get down to the business of dinner. Logan, Meg and Hadley followed with even more plates of goodies.

"Issa," Logan said then, "you haven't met Ian yet, have you? Issa, Ian. Ian, my sister Issa."

Issa and Ian exchanged nice-to-meet-yous, but Issa refrained from commenting on the twins' resemblance to each other because she thought they probably heard that too often.

Then to round out the introductions, Jenna said, "And the other one you don't know is over there— Abby. She's the baby my sister, J.J., had in high school. My niece—"

"And now her adopted daughter," Ian contributed.

"And soon to be Ian's adopted daughter, too, as soon as the paperwork is finished," Jenna said, smiling a beaming smile at Hutch's brother.

"I was sorry to hear about J.J., and about your parents," Issa said. Through her family she'd heard about all the losses that Jenna had suffered during the past year. Even though Issa had visited Northbridge periodically during that time, her visits hadn't coincided with any of the funerals and she also hadn't seen Jenna when she was in town, so this was the first opportunity to give condolences. In fact, neither Jenna nor Issa had lived in Northbridge until very recently, and Issa hadn't seen Jenna since they'd graduated from high school.

Jenna thanked her for her sympathy and Issa cast another, more concentrated glance in the direction of the sandbox. She felt obligated to show an interest in the child Jenna had made a point of telling her about.

Earlier when Issa, Hutch and Ash had arrived, Meg had informed the toddler that the other kids were out back. Ash hadn't wasted any time running through the place to join them. Now Issa spotted him playing in the sandbox with Issa's three-year-old niece, Tia; with Shannon, Chase and Hutch's twenty-month-old nephew, Cody, who Issa had met her first day back in Northbridge; and with a beautiful, curly haired baby girl who had to be Jenna's niece-turned-adopted daughter.

"How old is Abby?" Issa asked, too unfamiliar with children to have any clue.

"She's seventeen months," Ian answered in a proud voice.

"She's cute…" Issa said, unsure if she should be more gushy, if she should say or do anything else, and how long she should go on looking at the child before she could move on to other things. She was just no good at this stuff.

When Jenna thanked her for the compliment, Issa took that as her sign that admiring the child had gone on long enough and switched her focus back to the adults.

It was about then that the men moved nearer to the barbecue and the women migrated toward the picnic tables not far from there.

At the urging of Hadley, Issa sat beside her half sister on the bench. But as the other women began to chat about Jenna and Ian's upcoming wedding, Issa's mind and eyes wandered, and she ended up studying Hutch and Ian.

They stood side by side facing in her direction, watching Chase's grilling skills, and while she might not have remarked on the fact that the twins were near mirror images, it wasn't as if she hadn't noticed it. Now she couldn't help comparing the two.

They *were* almost identical. Only a few minor details made it possible to tell them apart.

Ian's eyes were a pale blue rather than the deeper, richer sky-blue that Hutch shared with Chase.

Both men's hair was the same length—short on the sides and back, slightly longer on top. But Ian's hair was just a shade lighter than Hutch's sandy-colored locks, and looked as if he put more effort into taming it, while Hutch wore the style with just a touch of bad-boy dishevelment.

And there was a difference in dress and comportment, too. There was something more formal and businesslike about Ian, about coming to a barbecue in slacks and a dress shirt.

But Hutch? He was wearing jeans and a long-sleeved T-shirt with the sleeves pushed to his elbows—definitely in keeping with the laid-back, casual air that invited everyone around him to loosen up, too.

No, there was nothing businesslike about Hutch as he talked and joked and made the other men laugh, and Issa knew almost instantly that if she were choosing between the two men—which, of course, she wasn't—Hutch would be who she chose.

Relaxed, personable, smooth, fun-loving—that was her impression of him. A guy who was easy to be around. Who other people were drawn to, too. The type of man who was sort of the yin to her yang.

Ah, but that was exactly why she had to be cautious when it came to her landlord, she told herself.

What she lacked in outgoingness, men like Hutch made up for. And in the past that had had its own appeal. Being with a man like that had provided her with a sort of camouflage to hide behind, a gap filler. But not only didn't that help her to improve upon her own shortcomings, but it also had actually led her to men with shortcomings themselves. Less obvious but far worse shortcomings than being a wallflower.

And she didn't want to risk the fallout that came from that ever happening again. So no yin and yang. No picking up the slack on anybody's part. No he-was-strong-where-she-was-weak/she-was-strong-where-he-was-weak stuff. Not for her. Not when the hidden weaknesses of the men she chose proved to be so disastrous.

It was a newly adopted conviction, but a conviction nonetheless, and she was holding tight to it.

Just then Ash got sand in his eyes and began to cry. Issa watched as Hutch crossed to his son with long, powerful strides, scooped up the little boy and commiserated with him while he rubbed his back.

"I know that hurts, big guy, go ahead and cry," he encouraged.

Issa's first thought was that commiseration and rubbing the toddler's back weren't going to get the sand out of his eyes.

Then she realized that it was the encouragement for the little boy to cry that was the solution—the tears were washing the sand away. And sure enough, within a few minutes the two-and-a-half-year-old was fine again.

Huh...

If she hadn't seen it herself, Issa didn't think that route would have occurred to her. Looking on, she'd thought Hutch should rush Ash into the bathroom and flush his eyes out with water. But the tears had been an easier solution and she filed that knowledge away for future use when she was dealing with her own child.

Then it struck her that in that way Hutch Kincaid could be a double whammy.

Not only did he seem to have the kind of personality that had historically been the yin to her yang, but he also had the abilities as a parent that she lacked. Abilities that could potentially compensate for her weaknesses on that count, too.

But being with an outgoing man had never made her more outgoing; it had merely masked the fact that she wasn't. And when it came to parenting, she thought that she had to guard against thinking that being with someone who was already a good parent would automatically make her a good parent, too. Or worst of all, mask the fact that she wasn't.

No, when it came to parenting, she had to do everything possible to *become* a good parent herself.

So yes, there were two reasons for her not to be memorizing every sexy little line that formed at the corners of his beautiful eyes when he laughed.

And if two reasons weren't enough, she could add one great big huge third reason, she reminded herself.

She was pregnant.

Admittedly, that tended to slip her mind because

it didn't seem real yet. But it *was* real. And what man would want a woman pregnant by someone else?

No man she knew.

And why was she even thinking anything like that?

Hutch Kincaid was her landlord, he'd fixed her door, he'd offered to carpool with her. There was nothing in any of that to require reminders of why she shouldn't or wouldn't or couldn't get involved with him and she wasn't quite sure how her thoughts had gotten there.

Except that he laughed again just then and that face of his lit up, and for a moment she couldn't help staring at him.

He was simply too good-looking.

But that wasn't important.

Hutch Kincaid was just a guy who happened to own her apartment, live downstairs and know some of the same people she knew. An incredibly attractive guy, but just a guy.

And she was nothing more than his unwed pregnant tenant—pregnant being the most significant part of that because if there was any man-repellent stronger than that, she didn't know what it was, especially because it had even repelled the man who had caused it.

So whether or not Hutch Kincaid showed signs of being the sort of man she had vowed to avoid, it didn't matter. She was protected even from herself.

Which was for the best.

She had enough on her plate as it was.

And yet...

There was something that made her a little sad to think that she'd been put on the shelf.

Particularly when it came to Hutch Kincaid.

* * *

"Thanks for covering for me at the start of tonight, with the wine," Issa said to Hutch almost the minute they were back in his SUV when the barbecue was over.

"Hey, it got me chauffeured," he answered with a laugh.

He was sitting in the passenger seat, angled toward the center console with an arm stretched across the back of her seat. Because Ash was in the car seat in the back, Issa thought that Hutch was sitting that way to keep an eye on his son. But so far his attention seemed more focused on her as Ash almost instantly fell asleep.

"I didn't even think about the drinking issue giving me away," Issa explained. "When it seemed like it might, I just froze. You really saved me."

"Anytime," he said. "You were pretty quiet all night, though. Did it throw you that much off your game?"

"Oh, no, that's just me," Issa lamented.

"The shyness..." he said as if just recalling that about her. "How does that work for a teacher who has to stand in front of a room full of kids and talk every day?"

"It took some work and a lot of shaky-voiced lectures during my student teaching to get me there, believe me. And lecturing still isn't one of my strengths. That's why I like to use as many demonstration experiments as I can and beef them up so the spotlight is more on the science than on me."

"Beefing up the experiments is what led to Gob-o-Goo."

"Right."

"But this tonight, it was just family and old friends,"

Hutch pointed out, still sounding somewhat puzzled by the evening.

"I'm not the boisterous McKendrick. I think the shyness actually came from home, from hating it when my mother would put us on display like we were her doll collection. So being with family doesn't make it much better. I got into the habit of shrinking into the background at an early age and relying on my brothers and sisters to be center stage, so that's still what I fall into when I'm with them."

"I know all about being put on display," Hutch muttered more to himself than to her. Then to her, he said, "Or was it worse tonight because of Ian and me?"

It had definitely been worse because of Hutch and all that had been going through her mind about him, but she wasn't going to say that.

Instead she hedged, "It might have been a little worse because of a lot of things. Like there were also kids, kids, kids everywhere..."

"And that was bad because?"

"Because it was glaring evidence that I don't know the first thing about them, or about taking care of them, or about what they need or when, or what makes them tick."

Hutch chuckled kindly. "That sounded a little panicky."

"Because I feel a *lot* panicky I must be doing pretty well hiding it, then," Issa joked even though it was the truth.

"You're panicked at the thought of parenthood?"

"Oh, sooo panicked! I've just never been a kid person. My mother made Hadley take care of the rest of us, so I never had to look after my younger brothers or Zeli. When I was a teenager, I didn't babysit like my friends did. I just don't know the first thing about kids."

"But you're a schoolteacher," he pointed out a second time, as if she were giving him conflicting messages.

"In a high school—they aren't kid-kids. They're teenagers. Three-quarters of the way to being adults. And I'm only responsible for teaching them chemistry. But a baby…" Issa nodded over her shoulder in the direction of the slumbering Ash. "A toddler? A kid? Feeding it, changing diapers, keeping it clean and healthy and thriving? Walking, talking, brushing teeth, potty training—I don't even know where to start."

"Didn't you want kids?"

"Not particularly. I mean I didn't plan to have them. I just sort of thought that if that biological clock thing ever kicked in, I'd know it and things might change. But that didn't happen and this…" She hated referring to the pregnancy too literally. "This was a birth control malfunction. It's taken a lot of soul searching for me to decide what to do and I've decided to go through with it, but I'm just hoping it's the right choice. And tonight, being around all those kids, made me wonder."

Like she was wondering at that moment why, for someone who didn't ordinarily talk much, talking *too* much was the problem with this guy. And telling him things she had no reason to tell him. *Birth control malfunction*—had she really said that?

She sighed audibly. "I don't know, I just kept watching what all of you did with your kids and thinking that I don't know any of it."

"You have some time to learn, to get ready," he said on a positive note.

"I'm not sure time will help."

Hutch did glance into the rear of the SUV then, at Ash, pausing the conversation for longer than seemed necessary.

Then he looked at Issa again and said, "How about a crash course? Would that help?"

She had the impression that he'd weighed those words before he'd said them, that that had been the purpose of that pause.

"A crash course?" Issa repeated because she wasn't sure what he was offering. If he was offering anything.

"In kids. In parenting, although I'm in no way an expert. But I know from my own experience that it isn't easy to step into those shoes, so I'd be willing to give you a couple of lessons. And the loan of some child-rearing books I still go to whenever I have a question. And there's also Ash. You could do some practicing on him so you can start to get used to kids, to being around the little ones and dealing with them."

She didn't know if Hutch had any idea how generous she considered his offer to be at that moment.

Taking her eyes off the road to look at him, she said, "Really?"

He shrugged as if it were nothing. "I'll make you a deal. The Realtor gave me a list of properties for sale in town so I could drive by them and decide if I want to see inside any of them before she sets anything up—"

"Marsha Pinkell? She gave me a list, too. Probably the same one because Northbridge is a small town and there aren't that many things available."

"All the better. I was going to say that you could help me find the places, but now it'll give you the chance to check them out, too. And while we're at it, I was also going to say that we could trade services—I'll do the crash course in parenting for you if you give me the guided tour of Northbridge and introduce me around, help me to start becoming part of the community."

"*I'm* not really part of the community—I haven't lived here since I went away to college."

"You're still a hometown girl. Jenna said you hadn't seen each other in years and years, but you picked right up where you'd left off with her. I'm betting that'll happen with everyone. In fact, it'll give you the chance to get it started, let people know you're back. Or is this too much to ask of a Bashful Betty?"

It was. But the stress of that was less than the stress she'd been suffering over the thought of becoming a totally unprepared and incompetent mother.

So she made a counter-suggestion.

"How about if rather than making a whole project of introducing you around, I just do it when the opportunity arises, like when we run into someone I know. I don't think I can promise to be your sole entry into Northbridge society, but I think I can give you a foot in the door."

"Fair enough. So it's a deal?"

Was it a deal? Issa asked herself as she pulled his SUV into the driveway beside her own, smaller version.

Turning off the engine roused Ash, who sleepily demanded, "Where Za-Za?"

"Za-Za?" Issa parroted.

"The floppy lion he sleeps with. Don't ask me why he calls him Za-Za, he just does," Hutch confided before he got out of the SUV, closed his door and immediately opened the rear one to lean inside to say to

Ash, "It's okay, buddy. I'll have you in bed with Za-Za in a minute."

Issa decided she could use that minute to consider the deal she might be striking with Hutch Kincaid.

Earlier in the evening she'd reminded herself to beware of this man because he was the kind of guy she knew she was susceptible to. And nothing about that had changed, she reflected as she got out of the SUV and went up to the house's main door to unlock it.

Plus she realized she was susceptible to Hutch in particular. If she weren't, during the drive home she wouldn't have been as aware as she had been of the scent of his cologne, of the heat of his body just a console away, of that long arm stretched across the back of her seat.

She wouldn't have thought so much about her hands being on the same steering wheel his hands had been on, or that she was sitting where he usually sat, and liking the sort of familiarity that seemed to breed.

She wouldn't have just spent the past few hours at the barbecue stealing every glimpse of him that she could steal, and then have been secretly pleased afterward to have him to herself again.

So was it smart now to sign on for spending more time with him? She pondered the question as she opened the door and waited for Hutch to finish getting his son out of the car. Because time would have to be spent with him if she showed him around North-bridge, if she showed him whatever properties were on the market, and if she had him teach her what to do with a kid.

But she did desperately need to know what to do with a kid. She couldn't deny that. And maybe if she learned a few things, if she got a little used to Ash, she might not be quite as terrified as she was of her own coming child.

And Ash would be there—the thought struck her as she watched the little boy collapse onto his father's broad shoulder and return to sleep almost the moment Hutch closed the SUV's door. A two-and-a-half-year-old chaperone but a chaperone nonetheless.

Hutch carried Ash up to the house and across the threshold, muttering a "thanks" to Issa for holding the door for them. She followed him in and closed it behind them.

Then they were standing in the entryway with the stairs to Issa's apartment directly ahead and the door to the lower half of the house that Hutch used to the right.

"What do you say? Deal?" he said again, returning to their previous conversation as if it hadn't been interrupted.

Oh, but his eyes were blue...

And the fact that she was lost for a split second in them should probably be a deal breaker.

But despite that, she heard herself say, "Deal."

It made Hutch smile—first the left side of his mouth followed quickly by the right.

Holding his son securely in one arm, he held out his other hand to Issa.

She was a bit slow in realizing that he wasn't reaching for her, maybe to slip that hand to her waist to pull her closer—because that was what flashed through her mind.

But it was a handshake he was suggesting. Merely a handshake.

She slid her hand into his. The feel of her palm

against his was all too nice. The fact that she was still gazing up into those sky-blue eyes, the fact that she was suddenly wondering what it might be like if he did pull her in closer, lean down and kiss her made her worry that she'd made a mistake not to say good-night to him tonight and have as little to do with him as possible from then on.

But because he didn't lean down and kiss her, because he only shook her hand and then let go of it just the way he should have, she felt relieved that no matter what was going on with her, he was keeping this where it needed to be kept—purely friendly.

"How does late tomorrow afternoon sound?" he said then. "I have a pile of work to do at the store, but if you aren't already busy around four-thirty or five, we can drive by some properties, tour the town, maybe grab some dinner?"

"Sure," Issa agreed, forcing herself to recall that while that might sound like a date of sorts, it wasn't. It was nothing but part of the deal they'd just struck— her knowledge of Northbridge in exchange for learning what to do with kids.

"Four-thirty or five, that's fine," she added. "How do you want to hook up—" Bad choice of phrases. She hurried on, hoping he hadn't caught it. "Do you want me to meet you at your store or come back here or—"

The slight hint of a chuckle said he had caught her slip of the tongue, but he just let it go and merely answered her question. "I'll come back here to get you."

"Okay." And maybe she ought to stop gawking at him. "I'll see you when you get here then."

She went up two of the carpeted stairs before she remembered to say, "And thanks again for the save with the wine."

"No big deal," Hutch assured her. In a voice that seemed deeper for some reason.

And why hadn't he gone into his apartment? Why was he standing there watching her?

And why did it seem as if she were catching him at something, prompting him to abruptly turn to his apartment door?

There were no answers in the quick "Good night," that he said, though.

"'Night," Issa answered, climbing the remainder of the steps to the second level and her own apartment door.

But as she let herself in, as she heard Hutch close his door downstairs, she couldn't help wondering if there was any chance at all that he'd been thinking about kissing her the way she'd been thinking about kissing him, if he'd been regretting that he hadn't when he'd watched her head up the steps.

Probably not, she told herself firmly.

Pregnant women did not get good-night kisses from new men in their lives.

And she shouldn't even be considering Hutch a *new man in her life,* she reprimanded herself.

That wasn't what he was.

He was simply a new *person* in her life. A new acquaintance. Possibly a new friend.

That was all.

And kissing him was most certainly not something she should be thinking about.

Not even fleetingly.

Because even if it had crossed his mind, he hadn't done it.

And he wouldn't.

And that was something she was just going to have to accept.

Along with the rest of the realities she was trying to learn to live with.

Chapter Four

"Nooze fie more min-its, Dad."

The morning routine. Hutch's alarm went off. Either Ash was already awake, laying in his bed waiting to hear it, or it woke him, too. Ash climbed over the safety bars on his new big-boy bed, charged into Hutch's room and bounded onto Hutch's bed.

Because it happened every morning and Hutch wasn't quite as enthusiastic a morning person as his son was, Hutch had instigated the five-minute snooze— he hit the snooze button on his alarm and Ash had to lay next to him or sit against the headboard and wait those extra minutes before pestering him to get up.

But the two-and-a-half-year-old never missed a morning warning that five minutes was all he was allowed and how the time was to be used—because if Hutch so much as opened his eyes, Ash wouldn't let him lie there.

This Tuesday morning was one of the mornings when Hutch kept his eyes closed but couldn't fall back asleep.

Instead thoughts of Issa McKendrick instantly popped into his head. Much the way he found himself thinking about her almost every other waking hour.

And even though he wished that would stop, he knew it wasn't likely when he'd be seeing more of her now that he'd gotten himself into looking at houses with her, touring the town with her and teaching her the rudimentaries of parenting.

Not that he was dreading seeing more of her. That was the problem—he wanted to see more of her. And even though he told himself it was the mother of all bad ideas, he still kept setting up the opportunities to do that—first carpooling to the barbecue and now these other things.

It's stupid, he told himself. He had Ash to concentrate on, and being a single father, and another new store to get up and running, and moving to a new place, and starting a new life, and trying to heal old wounds with the family. Now was not the time to get into anything with any woman.

And Issa was pregnant...

The topper. Because yes, that was the frosting on the cake.

But he just kept forgetting it all. The image of her would pop into his head or worse yet, he'd get to be with her or catch sight of her, and that was it for him. The reasons went right out the window and all he could think about was that pale blond hair or that skin or those eyes or that honey of a little body....

Well, that wasn't all he could think about.

He also wanted to kiss the woman so damn bad that he could hardly believe it.

Both last night and the night before, saying good-night to her, there hadn't been a single thing in the world that he'd ever wanted as much as he'd wanted to kiss her, not a single other woman he'd ever wanted to kiss as badly.

Sorry, Iris....

But it had been Iris who had kissed him the first time, before he'd ever even thought of her like that. And, of course, from there he'd loved kissing Iris. He'd loved Iris.

But this thing with Issa, this was something else. Something he didn't understand.

Maybe it was the fact that she was so off-limits. She clearly had a lot on her plate, too, and wasn't in the market for a man. A crib, but not a man.

Unless the man was the father of her baby, but she made that relationship seem like a done deal. Plus when her brother had rented the apartment for her, Dag had also said she'd been involved with someone in Seattle but that it was complete and total history, so she was moving back to Northbridge to start over.

Still, she was pregnant. And he had his own issues. Nothing was going to happen between them. She was unattainable.

Or safe?

Maybe that was it—maybe because she was safely off-limits something about that let things run rampant in him.

Nothing really made sense and he just guessed he didn't have an explanation so he was going to go with unattainable or safe—one was as good as the other.

As long as he didn't go with the urge to kiss her, it didn't matter.

And so far he was doing okay with that.

He just had to keep it up.

Oh, bad way to think about it….

He raised an arm and draped it across his forehead. It was tough but he decided that he had to relegate Issa to the status of the fifteen-year-old babysitter he'd had a crush on when he was ten—someone to admire and enjoy from afar and that was it.

Except that both of the past two nights when they'd said their goodbyes, Issa hadn't been so far away. She'd been within reaching distance. Touching distance.

And he'd offered a hand to shake on the deal they'd made just so he could touch her.

And he wasn't ten. And kissing a girl certainly wasn't foreign to him. And he'd wanted to do it so much that it had been almost impossible to recall why he couldn't, especially when he'd had a hold of her and he could have so easily pulled her close enough to do just that.

But he couldn't, he told himself firmly.

He couldn't and he wouldn't.

The alarm went off again and Ash pinched the tip of his index finger and shook it.

"No more 'nooze."

"I know," Hutch assured, reluctantly accepting that reality.

But getting out of bed wasn't all he knew he had to accept.

Continuing to fight the craving to kiss Issa was part of what he had to do, too.

Come hell or high water.

* * *

"Ya' gotta love this town!"

Issa laughed at Hutch's vigor.

They'd driven by the houses on the list that the Realtor had given Hutch and the few that were different on Issa's list. Then they'd had dinner at the local restaurant and pub—Adz—and walked up and down Main Street and through the campus of the local small college.

Hutch had promised Ash ice cream if he ate all the peas and carrots on his dinner plate, so they'd ended their tour at the ice-cream parlor.

With ice-cream cones in hand, they'd then crossed South Street to the town square. The overall-clad Ash ate his cone sitting in the sand that surrounded the swings and jungle gym equipment, while Issa and Hutch sat on a nearby park bench with the gazebo not far away. The strains of the barbershop quartet's rehearsal there provided background music.

It was the perfect early-June temperature, so there were a lot of people out and about, chatting with each other and enjoying the outdoors. There were children playing on the equipment and more kids riding skateboards and bicycles around the square, there was the music, and Issa did think it was nice to be back in Northbridge even if she hadn't commented on Hutch's appreciation of the place.

"Come on," he cajoled, "you have to admit this is great."

"It is," Issa agreed.

"It doesn't sound like you like it as much as I do."

"Maybe not as much, but I like it," Issa said, thinking that she was enjoying his company more than the charm of her hometown. Each and every glance she sent his way gave her the splendor of the man in a pair of just-tight-enough-but-not-too-tight jeans and a heather-gray Henley T-shirt.

"Are you missing Seattle?" he asked.

"I liked Seattle," she admitted. "But this is home and even though I'm glad to be back, it's still where I grew up, so this isn't as novel to me as it seems to be to you. Walking along Main Street, talking to people you pass by, ice cream in the square—to me this is just a summer night in Northbridge."

"I grew up in a very elite, gated community that opened onto the country club golf course. Just milling around there—the way most people are doing here— would have been considered crass and probably would have brought out security to make sure mischief wasn't afoot. This small-town thing has a whole different feel to it."

"You might not like it so much when you find out how little privacy you'll have here—everybody knows everybody, and everybody knows everybody's business."

"Oh, now that's the same where I grew up—gossip was the lifeblood, and it could make or break someone. Is that why you're keeping your secret? Because you don't want the news to make the rounds? And will it make you or break you?"

"There will be plenty of talk. And whispers. And a few noses in the air. But no, I don't expect to be shunned or anything. I'm not looking forward to any of that, but I'm keeping my secret for now because the situation is… Well, it's embarrassing. And I don't want my family to know until…" Issa shrugged. "I don't know, until I've gotten used to the idea, and it seems real to me, and I feel more okay with it. Then maybe I'll be better at handling everyone else's reaction."

Hutch nodded and let the subject drop, returning to the one before. "You said Sunday night that you were at loose ends in Seattle. But still, are you a little sorry that you didn't stay there?"

She didn't have to think twice to answer that. "No, leaving was for the best. I was at loose ends, but other things were tied up good and tight and so finished that it was better to get as far away as I could."

"I'm figuring you're talking about the relationship that—"

"Yeah," Issa said before he could take that any further. But she didn't offer more information, opting for her own turn at changing the subject.

"You grew up in an elite, gated community on a country club golf course, huh? Where?"

"We lived just outside of Billings. My father played football for Kansas, but Montana was still where both of my parents grew up and where they wanted to live. So my father spent what time he had to in Kansas during the season and off-season training camps, then came back here the rest of the time. But the family lived in Billings year-round."

"And you like Northbridge better than country club living?" Issa asked.

"Don't get me wrong—a full-screen movie theater in the house, a pool in the backyard, tennis courts, a golf cart to drive over to the country club if we felt like it—life was not hideous for the Kincaid kids. But yeah, I do like Northbridge better. I think it's a better place for Ash to grow up," he said with a glance at the boy, who had moved on from eating ice cream to filling the cone with sand.

"Even though you liked growing up the way you did, you want Ash to grow up differently?" she asked. There seemed to be something conflicting in what he was saying.

"I liked the perks of the way I grew up," he hedged.

"But there were other parts that you didn't like?"

He shrugged. "My dad was away a lot, but when he was with us, he was almost with us too much, at least with Ian and me. For Lacey it was a different story."

"How was he with you too much?"

"He was determined that his sons continue the football legacy of Morgan Kincaid, so he pushed us to play the minute we could hold on to the ball and run—there are home movies of Ian and I getting our first footballs when we were about Ash's age and Dad cheering us on to make touchdowns with them. Which meant that we both ended up trying to run with footballs bigger than our heads and fell flat on our faces."

"But you improved from there."

"We couldn't do anything else," Hutch said with a laugh. "Dad wouldn't have had it any other way. We were in training with him long before we were even old enough to play little league, then he drilled and grilled us all through that and all through high school football, then college."

"Did you not want to play football?"

"That wasn't an option, but I liked the game. I wanted to play. Liked playing. It's just that it was a game to me, and to my father it was way, way, way more than that."

"Sure, it built his empire."

"Yeah, but even so, it didn't seem to me that it should be the be all and end all of life, the way it is for my father. I don't want anything to be that important to me. So important that it overshadows what I have with my kid."

"You don't need to be in Northbridge for that to be the case," Issa pointed out.

"True, but I think the slower pace here will help keep distractions from Ash to a minimum. I won't lose hours commuting to and from work. When he starts school I'll be able to walk him there on my way to the store so we can talk. Things like that."

"I hear that your father is bringing football and his intensity for it to Northbridge with the training camp for his new football team."

"Right, the Monarchs."

"Logan says it's causing a lot of football fever around here and that everyone expects Morgan Kincaid to become a fixture. Aren't you worried that Ash could come under your father's influence and catch football fever himself?"

"I'm not worried about it, no. It isn't as if I'm anti-football. If Ash discovers that he has a passion for it, fine. I just want to make sure that I don't take anything more seriously than I take being his dad."

"You felt as if football was more important to your father than you were?"

"He'd deny the hell out of that, but yeah. And I had trouble taking the game as seriously as he did. As seriously as Ian did, too, so there were problems."

"But wasn't it you who ended up playing professionally? Not Ian?"

"Yeah, it was me who got the bid from the NFL at

the end of college, not Ian. That was kind of rotten for him because he always worked harder than I did. But I had more speed, better hands. I don't know why it came out that way, but it just did. I do know that Dad and Ian would have both been happier if it had been Ian."

"Why is that?"

"Dad would have been happier because Ian would have done it exactly the way Dad wanted it done. He would have been single-minded, determined, he would have devoted himself to it just the way Dad did."

"But you're the laid-back twin," Issa said. That was the impression she'd gotten the night before at the barbecue when she'd compared the two brothers.

"I am. And it frustrated my father, so he tried to get it out of me by pitting Ian and me against each other all the time, making us compete with each other. In the end, it was just ability that put me ahead of Ian, which was sad for Ian because he had such a thing for pleasing Dad."

"You didn't care about pleasing your father?"

Hutch chuckled wryly. "I took more the rebellious youth route. I might have played football, but when it came to my father's strict, straightforward, unwavering opinions about things, I pretty much did the opposite of what he told me to do. I drank. I partied. I kept vampire hours. I enjoyed the female attention that came with it all."

"What were his opinions about things?"

"He has very traditional values—he wasn't a playboy, he got married, he had a family, he paid back his own good fortune by giving and working for any number of charities and organizations."

"All admirable," Issa judged.

"It was. It is."

"But it doesn't sound as if you actually admired that, either," Issa observed.

"I did. I do. On the whole. It was just that what looks and sounds admirable has its own drawbacks. Some of what he did, what he dragged me and Ian and Lacey into, wasn't really good for us."

"Like what?"

"He wanted to be in public support of adoption because that's what he and Mom had had to do to have a family. Not only did they adopt Ian and me, but our younger sister, Lacey, too, and he wanted that to be well known to encourage other people to give homes to kids in need of them."

"Again, admirable," Issa said but with more reservation than she had before.

"Sure. But to show his support and encouragement of that, we were continually paraded around at charity functions, photographed for newspaper and magazine articles, everywhere, all the time, as the adopted children of football great Morgan Kincaid."

Ah, so that explained his comment the night before about knowing all about being put on display.

"Did you feel as if there was a stigma to it?"

"It definitely labeled us. It followed me all the way through my football career. Every time I did something newsworthy some reporter was bound to say it was almost as if I was Morgan Kincaid's real son. Or if I fumbled or something, there would be a remark about how I didn't have the great Morgan Kincaid's genes to back me up—something that got said about Ian, too, unfortunately."

"That's lousy for you both."

"Yeah, I wasn't ever wild for wearing the banner of adopted kid the way we had to and I definitely got ticked off when, even as an adult, things went back to that. But it still didn't really impact me as much as it did Ian. Ian hated being singled out as adopted even more than I did. He had this idea that we—he—had to earn his place as The Son of Morgan Kincaid. That's where Ian's drive to please Dad came from, and again, why it would have been better if Ian had been the one with more ability."

"Do you think your father was disappointed that it was you who had more skill?"

"No, not disappointed. It was just that rather than making sure I made all my football decisions the way he wanted me to—probably the way Ian would have—I ended up doing things the way I wanted. Which turned out to clash with my father's plans, so it caused some pretty big problems that split up the family. A split that lasted until just recently as a matter of fact. But things have gotten worked out now."

Issa thought that because he was talking in generalities he must not want to tell her more than that, so she didn't press it.

Instead, she asked, "Does Ash have a football?"

"Until my father bought him a big one, he only had one of those little spongy foam footballs that are age-appropriate. He picked it out himself because it was blue and he uses it to wash his toy cars when I wash the real one. But now, yes he does have a genuine, regulation NFL football. It was the first thing my father gave him when they met a couple of months ago."

"Ash is two-and-a-half and he just met his grandfather a couple of months ago?"

"The split in the family," he reminded her. He didn't go into details but continued to talk about the football his father had given his son. "I got a stand for it and it's on a shelf, waiting for Ash when he's bigger. If he wants anything to do with it."

"So no pushing."

"Nooo, absolutely not. If he wants to play, great. If he doesn't, that's great, too. And if I ever have any other kids, no rivalry, no competing against each other, none of that. I want Ash to grow up like this." Hutch poked his chin at the scenes all around them. "Low-key, relaxed, free to do his own thing, whatever that proves to be. Except not that! No! Don't do that!"

Confused, it took Issa a moment to catch up. A moment in which Hutch made a dash from the park bench to the sandbox where Ash had decided—after using the ice-cream cone as a container for sand—to go ahead and eat it, after all.

Ash at first protested, but Hutch cut him off by sweeping his son up to tuck him against his side and carry him facedown—much the way he had probably carried many footballs, making the toddler giggle with glee.

Then Hutch dropped the sandy cone into the trash receptacle as he returned to the park bench and Issa.

"This has been nice and I really do hate to cut it short, but—"

"I'm sure it's getting to be Ash's bedtime."

"After it's his bath time."

"No bas!" Ash insisted.

"Yes, bath!" Hutch countered as Issa stood.

Hutch softened the blow of his decree by spinning

around in the direction of his SUV to make his son giggle again.

Then Hutch, who was smiling broadly enough to let Issa know he was enjoying roughhousing with Ash as much as Ash was enjoying it, confided, "I better watch out or I'm gonna end up with ice cream down my leg."

Issa's gaze went instantly to Hutch's thigh where muscle strained the denim of his jeans.

Then to avert her eyes, she quickly looked down at her khaki slacks and the cream-colored sweater set she was wearing, and proceeded to brush imaginary cone crumbs off herself as they stepped onto one of the sidewalks that would lead them back to South Street where Hutch had parked.

"So you do know that no matter how it might look on the outside, not everyone in Northbridge is low-key or relaxed," Issa pointed out once Hutch had Ash snugly belted into his car seat and they were on their way home. "It isn't as if there's something in the water here that guarantees calm."

Hutch cast her a sideways glance of those blue, blue eyes. "No? Really?" he joked facetiously. Then without sarcasm, he said, "There's still a different atmosphere here. Like one big family. I like that. And Ian is based here now because of Jenna. I kind of have it in my head that maybe if I'm here, too—with the old man only popping in occasionally—Ian and I can put those old rivalries behind us, maybe get to just be brothers, get to know each other's kids, get to raise them all together."

"That would be nice. For both of you. It's a shame that brothers should grow up pitted against each other, but it's even worse that twins shouldn't be closer."

"But we're working on it. We can't help seeing a lot of each other here. To tell you the truth, Northbridge sort of opened up two avenues to me. It offered the opportunity for Ash to grow up knowing his family, and it also offered a place with a strong sense of community—that's something I want him to have. I want to make sure he feels connected to things and people outside of himself, outside of the Kincaids—a family-of-man kind of thing where it isn't as dog-eat-dog as it is in the city, as self-centered. Where people look out for and look after each other even if they aren't related."

"I can see how Northbridge has that," Issa said, marveling at how much thought Hutch had put into the bigger picture of raising his son. And feeling all the more inadequate herself. Not only was she completely at sea over what to do with her own child when it was born, she certainly hadn't given any thought to the bigger picture, to the kind of person she wanted that child to grow up to be.

"Did you always have a game plan for how you wanted to raise kids?" she asked.

Maybe the softness of her voice gave away how insecure and unsure of herself she was feeling at that moment because Hutch took his eyes off the road long enough to give her a warm, comforting smile.

"Nah! I never thought twice about raising kids until I had one. And even then I mostly thought it wasn't really my job until it was."

"Whose job was it before that?"

"I hate to admit it and sound sexist, but my wife's," he said. "What I did do with Ash before I lost Iris was just what she told me to do."

"Does that mean there's hope for me figuring these things out down the road?" Issa asked with a laugh.

"Hey, if I can, anyone can," he assured with a self-deprecating chuckle as he pulled into the driveway and turned off the engine.

Issa got out of the SUV while he took his son from the car seat and set Ash down on the lawn before he went around to the rear of the vehicle

"I'll get your impulse buy," he said as he opened the rear door.

Passing by the antiques store in the course of their tour of the town, Issa had spotted and fallen in love with a hand-carved hall tree. She'd intended to buy it and have it held until she could go back for it. Hutch had nixed that notion and insisted that they load it into the back of his SUV to bring it home tonight.

"Come on, Ash, let's go unlock the door for your dad," Issa said, holding out her hand to the little boy the way she'd seen his father do numerous times during their evening together.

She wasn't sure if the two-and-a-half-year-old would take it, but he did, and together they went up to the house. She opened the front door and they stood waiting for Hutch to bring in the hall tree.

Once he had, he set it in the entryway as Issa brought in Ash. Hutch unlocked his apartment door and opened it.

"I need to bring this up to Issa's house," Hutch said to his son.

"I can drag it up the stairs," Issa said.

"No, you can't. It's solid oak and too heavy for you." Addressing his son again, he said, "Go on in and get the guys ready for a bath. I'll be right back."

"The guys?" Issa repeated.

"Ash is an expert at getting dirty, but as you might have already guessed, taking a bath is not on the list of things he wants to do. But a bath in the disguise of water war—"

"Water war?"

"He fights battles with the tub toys while I sneak in a little soap and scrubbing. Right now Froggy and the Duckster are really at odds. I won't know until I get into the war zone whether or not Frank might be joining in tonight—there were threats of him lending a hand last night."

"Frank?"

"The captain of Tub Ship. He's been keeping to the sidelines, but he won't be able to stay neutral forever."

"It sounds complicated."

"It's also messy. Everybody gets a drenching, me included. But the job has to be done and distractions can be a parent's best friend."

"Lesson number one?"

"And speaking of lessons…" he said very mysteriously, leaving the words hanging in the air as he shooed his son into the apartment, left the door open and then hoisted the hall tree again to carry it upstairs.

"Tomorrow night is Ian's bachelor party," Hutch said as Issa followed him and lost her train of thought when her gaze got stuck on the back pockets of his jeans and she began to think instead of what a terrific butt he had.

Bachelor party…she reminded herself.

"Ian's bachelor party," she repeated, tearing her eyes off his derriere when they both reached the landing in front of her apartment.

"I can't bring Ash," Hutch was saying while she unlocked the door and opened it. "And I was thinking that you could get your feet wet with a little baby-sitting for me."

"Oh, I don't know about that," Issa said in sudden alarm.

"I'll have him fed, bathed and in his pajamas. The only thing you'll have to do is entertain him for about half an hour and then get him to bed. That basically means reading him a story and tucking him in. It's almost nothing, so it's a good place to start."

"Are there diapers and bottles involved?"

He laughed. "I've heard people say blood and guts with less horror. No, no diapers or bottles, but, uh, you will need to start there with your own bundle of joy, so you better get used to the idea."

He brought the hall tree into her apartment and set it to the side of the door before he turned to face Issa.

"For now, though, I'm thinking tomorrow night would just be a way of dipping a toe in the pond," he persisted. "Ash is about ninety-eight-percent potty trained and he hasn't taken a bottle in over a year. He does sometimes have accidents overnight, so he wears a pull-up kind of diaper to sleep. He'll already be in that when you get there. You'll need to tell him go to the bathroom just before bed, but that's about all you'll have to do with that. He can manage the simple stuff on his own."

"What if it isn't just the simple stuff?"

Hutch laughed again. "Okay, stop with the deer-caught-in-headlights looks. It won't be anything but the simple stuff, I promise. Simple stuff all the way around. You might even have a little fun because he's a fun kid."

She must not have seemed convinced because Hutch nodded then and said, "Okay, if it would make you feel better, I can take tomorrow afternoon off and we can get together to run through it so being alone with him won't scare you so much."

She did like Ash. And from what she'd seen, he wasn't helpless. Hutch could teach her a few things. Then if all she had to do when she was alone with Ash was read to him, tell him to go to the bathroom, then tuck him in and bide her time while he slept, she could probably manage. Maybe it would be that first step she needed to take to make her slightly more comfortable with kids and child care.

"Okay," she agreed reluctantly.

"Tomorrow at three? Then you can rest from the ordeal before you come back to do the actual baby-sitting."

He was kidding, but Issa thought she would probably be so stressed out that it would seem like an ordeal and she would need to rest and regroup before she could face Ash on her own.

"Plus, remember," Hutch added, "this is North-bridge. The bachelor party is just at Adz, so I won't be far away. One call to my cell phone will bring me running."

That helped. "Okay," she repeated with more confidence. Not much more, but a little.

"Re-ee!" Ash hollered from downstairs.

"That's ready," Hutch informed her. "The battle must be about to begin." Then, over his shoulder he called, "Start taking off your clothes, I'll be right there."

"'Kay."

"That means that he's now standing in the hallway

stripping down. It wouldn't occur to him to go back into the apartment to do it because I didn't say it," Hutch said.

The image of the little boy undressing in the exact spot where his father had told him to made Issa smile. Or maybe it was the fact that Hutch was looking at her, smiling at her, his attention still obviously on her despite the exchange with his son.

Hutch reached out and squeezed her upper arm. "It really will be okay, you'll see."

"You might want to teach Ash to dial 9-1-1 just in case," she joked.

Hutch's smile stretched into a grin. "I can do that," he said with a laugh, rubbing his thumb up and down her arm.

He was merely comforting her, she told herself. Showing support. The gesture didn't mean anything else.

It was just that his hand was big and warm and strong, and it gave her goose bumps she couldn't quite explain.

Plus they were standing so close that she could smell the scent of his cologne and it was going to her head.

And there were those eyes of his...

Sky-blue and looking down at her with something that might have been interpreted as appreciation if she didn't know that was crazy.

He's just being friendly.

I'm pregnant.

He's not going to kiss me.

And yet...

He also wasn't making any move to leave. Or to take that hand away from her arm. Or even to stop that tiny massage of his thumb that increasingly seemed like something more than support or comfort.

And he was studying her with an intensity that seemed more than friendly.

Was she imagining it because she wanted it to be true? Because she wanted him to kiss her?

She did want him to kiss her.

It wasn't only a matter of wondering about it tonight; it was something she was actually trying to silently will him to do. Something she was inviting him to do with the slightest elevation of her chin, with eyes that met his and didn't shy away.

But then it was Hutch who shied away.

He gave one tighter squeeze of her arm and let go, seeming to straighten up—even though she hadn't realized that somewhere along the way he'd leaned toward her—and he stepped out of the doorway and into the hall again.

"I'll be ready for you at three. Just come downstairs," he instructed.

"I will," she said, trying not to sound disappointed even though she couldn't help feeling that way at that moment. "And thanks for hauling my hall tree."

"Happy to do it," he said.

He raised the hand that had been on her arm to gesture goodbye and with an expression on his handsome face that she didn't quite understand, he retraced his path down the stairs.

"Pick up your clothes and take them inside," she heard him say to his son.

For the second time the image of the little boy taking his father's instructions so literally made her smile.

But not even the humor in that was enough to chase away the regret that was sifting through her.

She really had wanted him to kiss her.

And he hadn't.

But she still thought that he might have been tempted to.

And while it was small consolation, it was a little.

Just not enough to help her feel any less unkissed.

Chapter Five

"Ba' 'ream! Ba' 'ream, Dad! Ba' 'ream!"

The sound of Ash crying threw Issa into a panic.

She was alone with him and he'd been asleep only about an hour on Wednesday night—barely long enough for her to clean spilled milk from the cookies-and-milk disaster. Barely long enough to put the couch cushions back from the jump from sofa to easy chair after he'd shouted, "Wa'ch me fwi!" Barely long enough to clean the bathroom after she'd turned her back for two minutes and he'd used his toothpaste-laden toothbrush to scrub the floor. Barely long enough to pick up the toys he'd flung everywhere in search of Za-Za the lion to sleep with and the storybook he'd insisted that she read him before putting him to bed.

And now he wasn't asleep, he was crying "Ba' 'ream!" and calling for his father over and over again.

Issa stood frozen, unsure what to do, unsure if he

would be more upset when it was her, a virtual stranger, who appeared at his door. If he might freak out or something.

She'd done everything exactly the way Hutch had demonstrated that afternoon when he'd given her the run-through. Ash, however, had not behaved the way he had with his father when he'd participated in the let's-pretend game that Hutch had made of the demonstration. Ash had been far, far more excited when Hutch had left tonight, when Ash was alone with Pit-tee Itta, as he'd called Issa. He'd been rambunctious, in fact.

Nothing had gone the way it was supposed to have gone. And even if it had, nowhere in the demonstration or in the instructions Hutch had given for all contingencies, had there been any warning of what Issa was assuming *ba' 'ream* was—a bad dream.

And she felt as if she were in a nightmare of her own because she had no idea what to do....

"It's okay, Ash," she called from the living room, hoping that the sound of a female voice would give the child advance warning to remind him that his father wasn't there, that she was. Hoping, too, that that simple, long-distance assurance might be enough to calm the child down.

"Ba' 'ream!" he responded, sounding even more pitiful.

"I'm coming," Issa said then, knowing she had to go to him, but nervous about what to do when she did.

She'd left Ash's bedroom door ajar—the way she'd been told to—so she pushed it open slowly and poked her head into the night-light-lit room rather than rushing in and risking scaring him more.

"It's me, Issa. Remember? Your dad isn't here."

"Ba' 'ream!" the toddler repeated and because there was no additional fear in it, she took that as a sign that her being there wasn't more alarming for him and went into the room.

"You had a bad dream?" she asked quietly on her way to his bedside.

"Monsers!" he lamented miserably.

"You had a bad dream about monsters?"

"Uh-huh."

It was so sad.

And yet he was also so cute sitting up in his twin-size bed with the safety rails, dressed in his teddy bear pajamas, rubbing his eyes with tiny fists, his cherubic face damp with tears and his quivering bottom lip jutted out.

Issa sat on the bottom half of the bed where the safety rails ended and rubbed one of Ash's feet where it was tented beneath the covers.

Still clueless about what to do, she repeated, "It's okay. Look around, there are no monsters."

Rather than taking that advice, the two-and-a-half-year-old slipped out from under his sheet and blanket and crawled into her lap.

"Oh…" Issa said in surprise and some alarm of her own.

For a moment she merely looked down at him, her hands up in the air where they'd gone reflexively when Ash had finagled his way to her lap.

But they couldn't stay there.

Feeling stiff and hopelessly incompetent, she awkwardly brought hands and arms down around Ash.

If Ash recognized her hesitation, however, he didn't

show it. He just snuggled up against her as close as he could get.

"Okay," she said yet again, this time more to herself.

Hutch had warned her that Ash would use stall tactics to put off going to bed.

And Ash had done that—he'd needed an extra drink of water, he'd wanted a second story, he begged to show her his new tennis shoes.

Issa had followed Hutch's advice and not fallen for any of it.

Fleetingly now, she wondered if this could be another tactic.

But the little boy curled up against her, quieted by the two middle fingers he'd put into his mouth to suck on, gave every indication of someone who had been awakened from a sound sleep by a bad dream, so she rejected the idea that he was crying wolf.

On the other hand, if this wasn't a stall tactic and was genuinely a bad dream, was it something she should call Hutch away from his bachelor party for? Did this qualify as an emergency?

In her own initial panic, it had felt like one. And Hutch *had* said that once Ash was asleep he was usually out for the night, which wasn't true now. So maybe this was something to call him for.

But the worst seemed to have passed and what if she called Hutch, got him to come home and all he came home to was his son sound asleep again?

She didn't relish giving evidence to the fact that she couldn't even do the job that an average teenager could do.

So she decided to wait a few minutes. She even began to relax enough at having Ash in her lap to tighten her arms around him, to ease up on her stiff-backed posture, to rub his back the way she'd seen Hutch rub it when the toddler had gotten sand in his eyes.

Oh, so she *had* seen Ash cry before, she realized, recalling the sand incident. In her alarmed state, she'd forgotten about that. This wasn't the first time.

Now here she was, remembering what Hutch had done to comfort his son. Doing it herself. And it was working because Ash laid his head heavily on her chest and went as limp as a rag doll.

Very, very carefully, Issa lowered her head so she could see the child.

Sound asleep. Right there in her arms.

Relief made her wilt a little.

And then she thought, *But now what?*

She was afraid to move, to even take too deep a breath and risk waking him, startling him, making him cry again.

It felt kind of nice to be holding him the way she was, to have him so trustingly nuzzled against her. And she definitely didn't want to set him off again.

So she decided to play it safe.

To merely stay the way she was and let Ash sleep in her lap until his dad got home.

"There you are!"

Issa was never as glad to see anyone as she was to see Hutch when he poked his head into his son's room. And it wasn't only because Hutch looked so good in a pair of jeans and a V-neck sweater with a white T-shirt peeking from behind the V.

She'd heard him come into the apartment and

whisper-call her name as he'd worked his way through the place in search of her. But she couldn't respond and had had to wait until he found her—still perched on Ash's bed with the toddler asleep in her arms.

"I'm dying a little," she whispered very, very softly. "I've been sitting here like this for over an hour without anything to rest my back against and I can't feel my hands anymore."

"Uh-oh," Hutch said, his expression slightly perplexed.

He crossed the room and instantly rescued her by slipping his son out of her arms.

Issa part wilted, part collapsed forward and dangled her arms on either side of her calves, shaking the blood back into her hands before she sat up again and arched her spine to stretch it in the other direction.

Keeping an eye on her, Hutch laid his son at the top of the bed where Ash had been before he'd crawled into Issa's lap.

Issa slipped off the bed cautiously, embarrassed by the loud crack her back made when she did and trying not to groan from the lingering ache as Hutch covered his sleeping son who was undisturbed by the move.

With Ash tucked in, Hutch nodded toward the door, indicating that Issa should lead the way out into the hall. Hutch followed her, pulling the door closed all but an inch again.

"What happened?" he asked in a quiet voice as they moved on to the living room.

"He woke up shouting *ba' 'ream* and calling for you."

"Bad dream."

"That's what I gathered—about monsters—"

"Yeah, he has those every now and then."

"I didn't know what to do."

Standing in the center of the living room, Issa went on to tell him all that had gone through her mind, how Ash had come to be on her lap and why she'd spent the past torturous hour like a statue even as her body had cried out for reprieve.

Hutch held his hands up, palms out, and said, "I'm pretty good at getting the kinks out. Can I try?"

It was purely therapeutic, Issa told herself when she couldn't find the strength to refuse his offer. It wasn't that the prospect of having this man, in particular, touch her was just too appealing....

"Go ahead," she said, turning her back to him and dropping her head forward to keep her ponytail from interfering.

Unfortunately that also gave her a view of her front half and she realized that she'd made the wrong choice of clothes for tonight—khaki slacks and a gauzy blouse over a tank top. After a prolonged amount of time with Ash sleeping against her she was a wrinkled mess.

She was just making a feeble attempt to brush some of the wrinkles out when Hutch first laid hands on her.

And that instantly chased away wrinkle worries.

Big hands cupped her shoulders in a warm, powerful grip that felt too good to leave her thinking about anything else.

He pressed his thumbs into her abused muscles as he gently but firmly pulsed her shoulders back and forth at the same time, easing the tension out of her. She caught the moan that tried to escape her throat but couldn't keep her eyes from drifting shut as she gave herself over to his ministrations until she was putty in his hands.

As he worked his way down either side of her spine, it occurred to Issa that he'd sold himself short by saying he was merely *pretty good* at this. He was great!

So great that the medicinal value actually did almost balance out the more sensual pleasure of having his hands on her.

Almost.

But when that balance began to shift and she started to want his hands to do those same things on other parts of her body, she knew she had to put a stop to it.

"Much better. Thanks," she said, getting as far as saying the words yet unable to force herself to step out of his reach.

But two more deep kneads and he took his hands away, leaving her with such a sense of loss, such a deep desire to have his touch back again that it rocked her a little.

He, however, was unaffected because in a business-as-usual tone, he said, "Unless you have to rush off, I brought a bag of doughnut holes home to share with you."

"Doughnut holes?" Issa said, turning to face him once more and laughing because doughnut holes seemed like a strange thing to have returned from a bachelor party with.

And why *was* he back from a bachelor party so early? And without any indication that he'd been drinking?

"I walked home by way of the doughnut shop and that made me want doughnuts. But they were just closing up and this was all they had left."

He snatched a white bakery sack from the coffee table, then sat sideways on the sofa and patted the cushion in front of him.

"Sit down, rest your back, have some doughnut holes," he invited.

A wise woman probably would have given him a thanks-but-no-thanks and left, Issa knew. Especially a wise woman feeling the way she did at that moment— she wanted his hands on her again so badly that she could have begged for it.

But apparently she wasn't a wise woman because the next thing she knew, she was sitting on the couch, too. Also sideways but using the arm of the sofa as a backrest so she could face Hutch and choose a doughnut hole from the bag when he opened it and held it out to her.

At least she'd left a respectable distance between them—that was the best she could claim when it came to the wisdom, or lack thereof, she was showing.

"What are you doing home from a bachelor party so early?" she asked then, just before biting her doughnut hole in half.

Hutch shrugged. "You know, a bachelor party in a small town—tame stuff. I had a couple of beers and that was about all that was going on, so I decided to call it a night."

Issa did know about bachelor parties and even in Northbridge they very often got raucous. And they never ended at ten o'clock. In favor of doughnut holes.

"Were you worried about leaving Ash with me?" she asked.

"Nah," he said without hesitation, as if he honestly

hadn't doubted her abilities as a babysitter. "Being back here just had more of a draw for me."

Because of her? Was she reading too much into his words?

But Ash was sound asleep, so either she was the *draw,* or Hutch didn't trust her. And if he didn't trust her, was it likely that he would have suggested she sit with Ash in the first place?

So maybe she *was* the *draw.*

A wise woman would probably try not to think that.

So she tried not to.

But she had to nearly bury her face in the bakery bag and choose a second doughnut hole so that he wouldn't see the smile she was fighting because that was exactly what she was thinking. And liking the thought of.

"So…" Hutch said then.

Issa looked up to find him barely suppressing a smile of his own.

"I can't believe you sat there like that for over an hour because you were so terrified of a two-and-a-half-year-old waking up," Hutch said. "How bad was he before bed?"

Issa saw Hutch glance at the things she hadn't had the chance to clean up before Ash's nightmare—the building blocks Ash had stacked into a tower and then knocked over, the toy soldier that was still floating in the fish bowl on the end table and the net that Ash had brought out to throw around during his ten minutes as Spiderman—that was still draped over one arm of the chair.

"He was full of energy," Issa said, unsure whether a list of the things that had gone wrong made her or Ash look worse. "But I don't know what to do with a scared, crying kid, so once he was asleep again, I couldn't take any chances of him waking up."

"Uh-huh. And should I consider the level of chocolate you're needing right now—chocolate doughnut holes covered in chocolate frosting and chocolate sprinkles—a sign of how stressed out you've been?" he asked, failing to keep his smile under wraps now.

"If only I could dunk them in fudge sauce..." she joked, sinking her teeth into the second doughnut hole.

"Quadruple chocolate— Wow, he must have been bad," Hutch said, his smile stretching into a grin. "I'm sorry, he's usually a pretty easy kid."

"I don't think it was him," Issa admitted, defending the toddler. "It was probably just that I'm no good at the mom stuff."

"And tonight didn't build your confidence the way I hoped it might?"

She thought about that while she finished the doughnut hole. "I guess I *did* get through the night and weather the storm of a bad dream. That's something."

"It is," Hutch agreed, taking a second doughnut hole for himself—he opted for the simple glazed ones both times. "I probably should have warned you about the dreams. He doesn't have them that often, though, so I didn't think about it. But I'm guessing you just fell back on what your mother did for you when you were a kid and had a nightmare."

"*My* mother? My mother needed her beauty sleep, complete with one of those sleep masks like you see in the movies."

"A *sleep mask?*" he repeated in disbelief. "You said something before about your mother putting on airs— that seems like one of them."

"Oh, yeah. Right along with our *European* names. And poor Hadley got stuck being the *house staff*— maid, cook and nanny. But she was just a kid, too. She was only three when our parents got married, four when Tessa was born. So it wasn't as if she was particularly good at a lot of it. Our bedrooms were basically dorm rooms—all the girls in one, all the boys in another, with Logan having to take care of the boys. In our room if one of us woke up with a bad dream and woke up anyone else, whoever else woke up usually just grumbled that it was nothing but a dream, to be quiet and go back to sleep."

"Oh," he said as if he wasn't sure what else to say to that.

"Don't worry, that isn't what I did with Ash. He looked so cute and he was so sad, he broke my heart. I told him to look around and see that there were no monsters, and he did the rest on his own. But once he was in my lap, I didn't know what would happen if I moved him."

"So you do have some instincts even if you didn't get the chance to learn from the way you were raised."

Issa made a face. "It doesn't feel like I have any instincts for this at all. But I know I didn't learn anything from my parents."

"Neither of your parents?"

"My dad went to work, came home and watched TV. My mother was all about appearances—she gardened, she gave formal teas, she shopped, she had her hair and nails done, and it took a lot to keep her nose as high in the air as she was determined to keep it. The best I can say is that she didn't treat the rest of us the way she treated Logan and Hadley—she constantly called us the *real* McKendricks—and delegated Logan and Hadley to something much less than that and made them *earn their keep,* Hadley especially. But it wasn't as if she was warm and fuzzy to the rest of us, either."

"You were her doll collection…" She was surprised to hear him repeating something she'd said on Monday.

"More that than her kids. She'd dress us up and use us as another avenue for showing everyone in town how much better she was. If we were going to be seen—at church or any town function or even at home if she was having people over—there was to be no hair out of place, suits and ties on the boys, frilly dresses and white gloves on the girls, shoes shined, heads up, shoulders back, dignified and sophisticated—or at least what she considered sophisticated—at all times."

"And you think that's where your shyness came from?"

"I don't know if it came from that or if it was already a part of me that got worse because I was so mortified at being shoved into the spotlight to prove something. But I was definitely mortified every time. Then, behind the scenes, it was Hadley looking after us all. Maybe if that hadn't been the case, if I'd ever been given any of the jobs Mother insisted that Hadley do, I might have learned something and now I'd be more prepared for motherhood."

"And your dad didn't ever step in and tell your mother to treat Logan and Hadley better?"

"My mother ruled the roost, my dad watched television and didn't rock the boat," Issa said with a helpless shrug.

"I can't imagine that," Hutch said, sounding aggravated. "I know there can be problems with step-parents. I had enough friends who resented theirs to know it isn't an easy mix, and I worry about letting someone into Ash's life who won't see him as their own kid or treat him well. But the thought of sitting by while it happens, while someone *mis*treats him—" Hutch shook his head "—I think I'd come unglued. I know I wouldn't let it go on."

"It might have helped a little that Mother wasn't any nicer to the rest of us—not that I'm excusing the rotten stepmother stuff, because I'm not. But in its way it made all of us kids close. Logan and Hadley had to do so much taking care of the rest of us that they were more like the real parents. I never think of Logan or Hadley as *half* siblings, but there was a lot of distance between us kids and our parents, and I'd never say I was close to either my mother *or* my father. It was more like the seven of us were the family and our parents were just the figureheads."

"But that isn't what you want to be to your own kid, right?"

"I don't want to be the kind of mother mine was, no," Issa confirmed without having to consider it. "I just don't know how to be any other kind, either."

"Well, tonight you were the kind who sacrificed your own comfort to make sure Ash wasn't afraid so he could get some sleep."

Issa made another face. "I wish I could take that credit, but it was just that I was scared stiff that he'd wake up and cry again and I wouldn't know what to do."

"Still, what you ended up doing was to Ash's benefit, not your own, and at your own expense." He aimed his dented chin at her and said, "Speaking of which, how is your back?"

If she said it still hurt, would he rub it some more?

It was tempting.

Too tempting. And she knew she had to resist that temptation. In fact, she knew she should get out of there before the temptation got any worse.

So she said, "It's okay. I think all it needs now is to be laid out flat on a mattress."

Oh, that hadn't come out right!

"I mean, I should get upstairs and go to bed," she amended, her cheeks hot with embarrassment.

Hutch was grinning at her again, so she knew he'd caught her blunder but he let it pass and merely held the bakery bag out to her once more. "Want to take the rest of these?"

"No. If I do, I'll eat them all. Besides, Ash didn't get any. Save them for him."

"See? Thinking of him and of what he'd like—that's something a mom would do," Hutch said as Issa stood and headed for the door.

Even though he joined her there, she decided not to remind him that she'd thought of herself initially and Ash only after the fact. But it was something she was aware of herself and it made her worry again that she might not be able to be a put-the-kid-first parent.

"So now that we have this thing rolling," Hutch said at the door.

"What *thing?*" Issa asked, pausing with her hand on the knob and thinking that she might have missed something.

"The you-learning-the-ropes-of-child-care thing," Hutch explained. "You got your feet wet tonight, how about we keep it going tomorrow? I'm taking Ash out to Jenna's farm in the afternoon so he can see the animals and ride the pony she just got. Then maybe we can have dinner and you can advance from bedtime cookies and milk to overseeing a full meal?"

He didn't know that the bedtime cookies and milk had been a disaster. And she didn't want to tell him.

She also didn't want to pass up the chance to see him tomorrow.

Which was not a good sign.

Even if it might serve the purpose of teaching her how to avoid things like tonight's spilled milk.

"What time?" she heard herself ask even as she was having that internal debate. "The obstetrician I'll be using is in Billings, but she comes to Northbridge one day a week and uses the family practice doctor's office to see patients here. I have an appointment with her at three—hopefully without anyone noticing that that's what I'm doing and starting any talk around town."

"I was going to work until about two or two-thirty. Why don't I pick you up and take you to your doctor's appointment? That way, if anybody sees us, you can say we're there so I could drop off Ash's records for the family practice doctor. Then we'll go out to Jenna's."

"You'll cover for me again?" Issa asked, looking up at his handsome face and thinking that this guy might just be too good to be true.

He shrugged those broad shoulders the same way he had when he'd insisted the bachelor party was lame. "It's nothing," he claimed.

Except that it was something to Issa—it was someone looking out for her, being nice and thoughtful, helping her and making her feel less alone in her current predicament.

"I really appreciate it," she told him, aware that he didn't have any idea how many things she was clustering into that appreciation.

"No big deal," he assured.

She didn't know why his voice was suddenly deeper, more quiet, almost intimate. Or why he was looking at her the way he was looking at her—studying her face, peering into her eyes. She only knew that she was a little lost in that gaze, in returning it and drinking in the sight of his chiseled features.

Then he reached a hand to her upper arm and squeezed it. "You did well tonight with Ash, whether you know it or not," he praised.

Issa thought that he might change his mind if she'd missed cleaning up any of the milk on the kitchen floor and his bare feet stuck to it later.

But she didn't say that. At that moment she didn't actually care about her abilities, or lack thereof when it came to child care. That was the last thing on her mind as she stared up into his sky-blue eyes and thought only of the man standing there with his big hand on her arm.

What was on her mind at that moment was the memory of how it had felt to have his hands on her back earlier, how much she'd wanted to feel them on other parts of her body, too.

How much she wanted that all over again now.

How much she wanted it to happen while he kissed her, because yes, that was also on her mind again tonight.

What was there about this man?

But just as she asked herself that question, Hutch

leaned forward and did kiss her. A very quick, very light, not-really-more-than-friendly kiss. On the cheek.

And yet it was still enough to set her all a-tingle.

"Thanks for baby-sitting," he said, tightening his grip on her arm for another split second before he released it.

"Sure," Issa muttered, opening the door then because that seemed like what she should do. "See you tomorrow," she said as she went out.

"I'll be here to get you a little before three."

"Okay," Issa agreed.

But as she climbed the steps to her apartment, she had to wonder what was going on with both of them.

With Hutch for cutting out on his brother's bachelor party to spend the time with her instead.

With Hutch for that back rub that might have been a little above and beyond the call of duty.

With Hutch for just having kissed her, no matter how platonically.

And with her.

With her for coming very near to being turned on by that back rub.

With her for being so relaxed with him, for talking so freely, for being so thrilled with the idea that he might have cut his brother's bachelor party short to be with her.

With her for so many nights now of imagining and wishing and wanting him to kiss her, and then being both titillated by that nothing-of-a-kiss he'd given her and feeling disappointed that it hadn't been more than a nothing-of-a-kiss.

With her for losing sight of the fact that she was

pregnant every time she was with the man and behaving as if she wasn't.

But wondering about it all didn't give her any answers as she let herself into her own apartment.

And the only thing she actually took inside with her was the lingering sensation of Hutch's lips on her cheek—warm and soft and smooth with the faintest hint of roughness where his chin had brushed her skin.

The lingering sensation of that kiss and an even deeper yearning for a better, longer, genuine kiss.

On the lips.

From him.

The man she had no business wondering about or wanting or wishing for kisses from.

The man she had no business with at all.

Chapter Six

"Dad and big brother can come back, too."

For a moment Issa didn't know what the nurse was talking about. Then she realized that the young, round-faced woman was referring to Hutch as *Dad* and Ash as *big brother*.

Embarrassed, Issa shot a glance at Hutch, who had remained sitting in the waiting room chair when she'd stood at the sound of her name.

He smiled a serene smile, undisturbed by the assumption the nurse had just made. "I can play stand-in," he offered in a whisper.

"Oh, no, that's okay," Issa said, hurrying for the door to the examining rooms where the nurse waited. "He's just a friend," she told the nurse when she reached her. "And the little boy is his."

"He's a cutie," the nurse said.

Hutch or Ash?

"Both of them," the nurse added under her breath as if she'd read Issa's thoughts. Then, when the door was closed between the two sections of the office, the nurse said, "Is Dad married? I didn't see a ring."

Issa took an instant dislike to that nurse. And rather than answer the question, she said, "Which room shall I go to?"

"Ah, maybe not *just* a friend," the nurse muttered as she led the way to an exam room. "Have a seat. I need to get the laptop to take your history," she said with a knowing smile before she closed the door and left Issa alone.

And steamed.

That was a lot of gall, she thought of the nurse's blatant interest in Hutch.

But she also knew that it shouldn't have bothered her. It shouldn't be bothering her still. She shouldn't be sitting there wondering if the nurse had made a beeline back to that waiting room to flirt with Hutch. Or be aggravated by the idea.

Maybe not just friends.

The nurse's words echoed through Issa's head.

Just friends, and barely that—no one could make a case for Hutch being anything more. Well, he was also temporarily her landlord, but that was nothing. And neither was the kiss on the cheek the night before; he could have kissed his grandmother the same way.

Yet she had to admit that when it came to her other male friends—guys who really were *just* friends—she didn't have the kind of thoughts, the kind of feelings, the kind of urges she was having for Hutch.

She certainly wouldn't have wanted to scratch another woman's eyes out for showing an interest in one of them. She would have encouraged it. She *had* in the past encouraged something similar to that when the new art teacher had asked her if Sean, the other chemistry teacher, was single. Issa had gone so far as to set the two of them up.

But now she was just itching to go back to that waiting room and make sure the nurse wasn't out there with Hutch.

Hutch, who would have come back here with her to lend her support if she'd taken him up on his offer.

There just wasn't anything *not* to like about him. So yes, she liked him. Too much to hand him over to some cheeky nurse.

But she didn't really have the right to stand in his way, she reminded herself. He might like the nurse. Ash might also like her. They might all hit it off. Hutch might fall madly in love with her, marry her and the three of them could live happily ever after....

Why did she hate that idea so much? Issa asked herself.

But, oh, boy, did she hate that idea!

She was sitting in an obstetrician's office waiting to meet the doctor who would deliver the baby she was pregnant with by someone else, and going crazy with the thought of Hutch Kincaid finding happiness with another woman.

Crazy—she was right about that. She'd gone out of her mind.

But she couldn't deny that she was attracted to Hutch, so she might as well stop trying. She was wildly attracted to him. How could she not be? He was drop-dead gorgeous, nice, personable, kind, funny, fun to be with and a good father. And he was sexy—she couldn't deny that, either. He had so much appeal—sex and otherwise—that it was impossible to overlook.

But what she did keep overlooking again and again was the fact that she was pregnant. And she needed to stop overlooking it.

It was just that she didn't *feel* pregnant. Her stomach was still flat. She wasn't sick. She hadn't developed any sort of sense that anything had changed, or even any maternal instincts that might make the world take on a rosier hue. With the exception of a little dizziness now and then, needing some extra rest and a bigger bra, she felt like her same self.

And maybe that was part of the problem. If she *felt* pregnant or maternal or any different than she ever had, maybe it would be easier to be thinking about that than about Hutch.

But as it was, it was only Hutch on her mind night and day.

She had to curb that, she told herself. She could be friends with Hutch, but that was all.

And that was all he wanted, too. If anything proved that it was last night's kiss on the cheek—something platonic and passionless.

And so, so disappointing.

But exactly as things between them needed to be and would stay.

So if the nurse hadn't gone out into the waiting room and taken things into her own hands, Issa told herself that she should offer to introduce them.

She should...

But when the nurse came back into the room to take her blood pressure Issa didn't do anything of the kind.

Instead she remained stony, barely cooperative, less-than-friendly.

And really, really resentful of the fact that the nurse was apparently as free as a bird if she wanted to put the moves on Hutch Kincaid.

While Issa was anything but.

"All's well?" Hutch asked as they left the doctor's office.

"I'm barely two months in, but so far, so good, it seems," Issa answered. "Today was just talk, a couple of lab tests and that was about it. The doctor I saw in Seattle did an exam and sent my records, so this was just to get things started with the new OB. There's not really much to say or do at this point."

And she didn't want to talk about it.

Hutch must have gotten the message because he changed the subject as they reached his SUV and he hoisted Ash into the car seat. "Ian called my cell phone while you were in with the doctor. He's leaving work early so he can be at the farm when we get there. He and Jenna invited us to stay for dinner tonight."

"Oh. Maybe you should drop me off at home, then. I don't want to butt into a family dinner."

With Ash securely strapped in, Hutch backed out of the SUV to glance at her with raised eyebrows. "Wow, do you always tense up that quick at just the idea of dinner with friends?"

The man was too perceptive.

"It isn't really dinner with friends. Jenna and I may have both grown up in Northbridge, but we didn't know each other well, and it's been years and years since we've seen each other—we're closer to strangers than to friends. When I thought she might be showing us around her farm I figured that would give us something to talk about. But dinner after that—"

"And my brother *is* a stranger, and there would be conversation and here you are without crib notes," Hutch teased her, making light of her discomfort.

"Come on," he coaxed. "You would definitely not be *butting* in because you were *invited.* In fact, when I called Jenna this morning to tell her what time I'd be out there, I told her I was bringing you. The dinner invitation came later, so maybe they want you there more than me."

"I'm sure *that's* not true," Issa said as he opened the passenger door for her because she was so distracted that she'd forgotten about getting into the vehicle herself.

"Hey, things with my brother are on the mend and we're both trying to figure out how to have a relationship that doesn't involve us being competitors, but we aren't there yet. It's not beyond the realm of possibility that a foursome for dinner would seem better to him than a threesome at this point. I know it would make it easier for me…" he added with an engaging grin that told her he honestly did want her along.

Then he said, "I promise we won't stay the whole evening. I need to get some paperwork from the store before we take Ash home to bed, so we have an excuse to leave right after dinner. And I'll carry the ball while we're with Jenna or Ian. If there's the slightest lull in the conversation, you can count on me to fill it."

She was definitely right about him—handsome-as-all-get-out, nice, sexy, personable, easy to be with, funny and worst of all, the perfect counterbalance of strong-where-she-was-weak. It was the most dangerous of combinations for her and she knew it. And that was all the more reason she should insist on going home right now, on not seeing any more of him, on handing him over to the brassy nurse.

Then he said, "Besides, you can still do some practicing at taking care of Ash. Plus Jenna has Abby and Abby is eight months younger than Ash—that means she's more on the baby side than the toddler side. Not only can you watch Jenna with Abby and learn from that, but you could also even volunteer to change a diaper."

"Let's not get carried away," Issa said with a revolted laugh.

"But," he went on, "my plan was to have dinner with you tonight, so if you don't want to stay there after we do the farm experience for Ash, I'll just tell them no and we'll do something else, the way we would have otherwise."

Her choices were to either go or throw a wrench into the works of Hutch and his brother reconfiguring their relationship.

Issa didn't want to do damage.

And she *was* trying to learn parenting skills, which meant that watching Jenna with Abby could be a lesson for her.

"Okay, okay, dinner with Jenna and Ian," Issa finally agreed, trying not to feel as if she were part of a couple having dinner with another couple.

All the while feeling secretly pleased that Hutch was willing to turn down dinner with his brother in favor of dinner with her.

"Great! I'll call and tell them we're on our way and

we'll stay," Hutch said as Issa got into the SUV. "Maybe we'll pick up a cake at the bakery or something for dessert."

We, we, we...

All very couple-ish.

And while Issa told herself not to think about that as Hutch closed her door and went around to the driver's side, while she told herself to keep everything in perspective, to remember that they absolutely were *not* a couple and never would be, to be wary of just how comfortable she was with him already despite the fact that he wasn't too much more than a stranger, she couldn't help glancing at the building they'd just left and thinking of the bold nurse again.

Issa knew that she was playing with fire when it came to Hutch and that she should stop.

But still, there she sat, glad it was her in his passenger seat and not the nurse.

Ash loved the farm. He oinked to the pigs, he petted the cows' noses, he chased the chickens, he rode the pony, he fed carrots to the full-grown horses and he even made friends with the barn cat that was at first leery of him.

He was slightly confused about the difference between the farm and the zoo because he repeatedly said, "See muckies now," and had to be told that there were no monkeys. But Issa could tell that he was enjoying himself anyway.

In the course of it all, Hutch looked on and gave instructions and warnings, but for the most part he stood back and let Issa handle Ash.

Issa was surprised by how much fun she had with

the toddler and the animals, and by her own skills when it came to foreseeing potential dangers and avoiding or averting them before anything happened. It was as if she had kicked into a different mode that made her more alert, more aware of everything, and also more attuned to what was most likely to catch the little boy's interest.

She could tell in advance that he was going to try to scoot under the fence railing and get into the muck with the pigs, and she caught him before he had the chance.

She saw Ash aim the carrot for the horse's nostril and stopped him before he did something he shouldn't do, redirecting him to let the horse take the carrot from him.

She saw him rush the barn cat and caught him before he alarmed the tabby, coaching him about how to entice the animal to come to him instead.

By the time the petting zoo portion of the visit was over Issa did feel marginally less useless around kids. In fact, while Ash and Abby dug in the flower beds and the adults sat on the front porch having lemonade and chatting, Issa reflected on how brilliant Hutch was at initiating her into the whole business of raising a kid.

Then came dinner and that took some of the oomph out of her fledgling confidence.

To explain to their hosts why she was feeding Ash, Hutch said she'd lost a bet and that was how she was paying it off. Then, with Ash seated between them at the table, Hutch faced in the opposite direction to talk to Ian about breaking ground on the training center for their father's football team.

It was cookies and spilled milk all over again.

Either the country air had given Ash a voracious appetite or he loved lasagna as much as he loved the farm, but Issa couldn't feed him fast enough. He plunged his hands into the lasagna and came out with fistfuls of ooey, gooey cheese and sauce and noodles that he smeared all over his face in his efforts to get the stuff jammed into his mouth. He dropped it down the front of him, on the table, on the floor, smeared it on the handle of his sippy cup when he decided to wash it down with a drink of milk, and generally made an enormous mess.

Issa was glad she'd worn a short-sleeved shirt because while she was trying to lean back out of harm's way, her hands and forearms were still splashed, and only the napkin across her cream-colored linen slacks protected her. The entire area around Ash's booster seat ended up wearing almost as much lasagna as Ash's face did.

It was Ian who finally glanced across the table at her struggles with the two-and-a-half-year-old and said to his brother, "How big a bet did she lose to you?"

Only then did Hutch notice what was going on. He took one look and laughed. "Not *that* big," he said, pivoting in his chair to take over.

"I wondered how long it was going to go on," Jenna said with a laugh, getting up to grab some paper towels to dampen and hand to Hutch.

From then on Hutch dealt with his son, leaving Issa to watch how Jenna handled Abby, and admire the ease with which Jenna got the baby fed, cleaned up and generally taken care of.

By the time Issa and Hutch left, Issa was again convinced that she was going to be the worst, most inept mother on the planet because she didn't think she would ever gain the kind of calm skill both Jenna and Hutch had.

"It just takes time and practice," Hutch assured her when she told him as much on their drive back into town.

Issa wished she believed that.

Back in Northbridge, Hutch stopped at the site of the newest Kincaid's All Sports to pick up some paperwork.

As he parked in front, he explained that not only had he bought out Northbridge's original sporting goods store along with all of its inventory, but he'd also purchased the vacant building beside it. He'd had the two structures joined to accommodate this latest branch of his chain.

"Come in and see what I'm doing."

Issa was curious and didn't hesitate to join him as Hutch took the now-cleaned-up Ash out of the car seat.

"I'na pay!" Ash announced as Hutch unlocked the front door to let them in and set his son down inside.

Issa gathered that *pay* was *play* when Ash ran for a section of the store that seemed already finished—an area cordoned off by a border of brightly colored miniature beanbag chairs.

"My brainchild," Hutch said with a poke of his chiseled chin in that direction. "It's a play area for kids. Parents can leave them there while they shop and the kids get initiated into some different sports."

"Ah, very smart. You're building a future client base," Issa said as she took in the sight of a short basketball hoop and backboard, the setup for T-ball, the toy tennis rackets and tiny golf clubs, the collection of foam footballs and baby barbells and various other brightly

colored sports-oriented toys and equipment. Ash leaped
onto the small trampoline built into the floor and began
to jump as gleefully as if he were on a bed.

"*Very* smart," Issa repeated when she realized that
a trampoline in the floor allowed kids to jump to their
heart's content without the danger of their falling off
of anything.

Hutch shrugged away the praise. "Ash likes it all, so
if nothing else, it keeps him busy."

"Still, it really is good business. Not only does it
give parents the chance to shop without the kids bothering them, but kids could potentially play with something and discover an interest or an ability they didn't
know they had before. Then parents might buy them
the equipment for whatever it is, and if that's just the
beginning of something, the kid could potentially grow
up to be the next tennis or football or baseball or basketball star and keep coming back to you for clothes
and shoes and everything else."

"Potentially," he confirmed.

"So Ian isn't the only Kincaid with business sense."

"Mine didn't come quite as naturally as Ian's did,
though. If it wasn't for my late wife none of this would
exist. The business was her idea and at first I was really
just the face on it."

"But now you're on your own with it and you seem
to be doing well," Issa observed.

"Still, it was Iris's influence that got me to step up
my game when it came to the business. That's the problem with football being easier for me than for Ian, I
think. I could afford to be lazier."

"Does that mean you were *too* laid-back?"

"It does, especially when it came to everything that

wasn't football. But Iris wouldn't stand for it and sort of kicked me into gear. Luckily."

"But it stuck," Issa said, choosing the positive view of something he seemed reluctant to take credit for.

"With the exception of one lapse that I shouldn't have let happen, it did, yeah."

Issa wasn't sure what that meant, so she merely said, "And now there will be five stores when this one is up and running."

"Right. Want the grand tour?"

"Sure," Issa said.

While Ash continued to jump on the trampoline, Hutch walked Issa through the open space. There were still some finishing touches needed on the construction, but the store was already in the beginning stages of being stocked.

Not being sports- or business-minded, Issa was more interested in watching Hutch than in what he was pointing out to her.

He was wearing a white polo shirt that he'd somehow managed to keep clean despite the lasagna debacle. It fitted him with no room to spare, which meant that it stretched taut across broad shoulders, expansive chest and back and muscular biceps.

His jeans were the ideal showcase for his perfectly shaped derriere, and he was wearing a pair of cowboy boots that had too many years on them to make her think he'd purchased them with today's farm experience in mind.

Altogether the look made her want to dub him the preppy cowboy and that thought made her smile a smile that had nothing to do with the workout equipment he was showing her.

"It's called a Pec Deck. Want to give it a try?" he asked, apparently misinterpreting the smile.

"Oh, sure," she said to keep up the image. Then to further the cause, she added, "I was just wondering if I had the strength to actually make it work."

"The weights in back control how hard or easy it is," he explained. "Then you just sit here like this—"

He positioned himself on the small padded seat that formed an *L* with the tall, narrow padded back and headrest behind it.

"Then you curve your arms under these—"

There were vertical pads attached to metal bars that came out from high up and behind either side of the backrest.

"Press your forearms to the pads, grab the top of them with your hands, then you just bring them and your elbows to the center and take them back again…"

He showed her. And again it was impossible for Issa to pay as much attention to the machine as to the man operating it.

Hutch sat up tall and straight, his biceps bulging from underneath the arm pads. And his pectorals? Wow. Her mouth went dry with the vision she had of well-honed muscle flexing beneath his white T-shirt.

And all she wanted to do was press her palms there so she'd know if they were as rock-solid as they looked.

"Okay, your turn," he said when the demonstration was over. "I'll adjust it to the minimum weight. It won't even be as much as lifting a bag of flour, so it shouldn't strain anything important."

When he got up from the seat, Issa took his place. Again she had to play along to conceal what was really going through her mind.

The seat was deliciously warm from the heat of his body, but she tried to ignore that and recall how she was supposed to position her arms.

Oh...

Talk about showing off her newly expanded chest! There were those B-cups poking out high and proud.

But there was no way to slump on that machine, so there was nothing she could do about it.

After adjusting the weights in the back, Hutch came around to stand in front of her.

And he saw. She knew he did. Not that there was more than an almost-infinitesimal glance downward before his gaze went to each arm in turn, but still.

Issa was just glad that the camp shirt wasn't knit because she felt her nipples tighten up and she wouldn't have wanted him to see *that*.

He smiled then. What was going through his mind about her? Was he amused by her technique?

"Don't just hang your arms there." He stepped closer. "Get a good tight grip and use your forearms and chest muscles to push."

Did she *have* chest muscles?

She didn't ask.

She didn't care. Especially not when Hutch came in close enough to clasp his hands over hers to bring them more firmly around the tops of the arm pads. Then he rested his forearms against hers and used them to show her what to do.

But once more, exercise was not on Issa's mind. She was lost in the sensation of his bare arms running the length of hers, of his powerful hands cupped over hers, of the heat of him and the scent of his cologne, of his chest so near that she could have pressed her face to it.

Which was more what she wanted to do than exercise.

But after one demonstration he let go of her and took a step backward.

Which didn't put him far away, but still left her more on her own that she wanted to be.

Issa inhaled and exhaled deeply, hoping to clear her mind. Then she tried to do the exercise Hutch had just done so effortlessly and found it more difficult than she'd expected, coming up short on her first go-round.

"I'm a wimp!" she said.

Hutch laughed—and she liked the sound of it too much to care if he was laughing at her.

"You really are," he teased. "Think about what you're doing this time and actually push. Don't just smack your arms up against the pads. *Use* your muscles."

"I might have left those home tonight, not figuring I'd need them," Issa said. But she did take his advice and manage to bring the arm pieces together and release them with an "Ugh" that again made Hutch laugh.

He stepped nearer and clasped her hands in his once more, this time to stop her from trying the exercise a second time. "I'm not so sure you *should* do this if it's that tough for you," he goaded.

Issa liked that he was so close, liked that he was touching her too much to try to prove him wrong. Instead she said, "*Mental* muscles are what you need to teach chemistry, not physical ones."

"Good thing," he teased, standing still and looking down into her eyes, holding them with his.

Then, when she least expected it, he leaned forward and kissed her. A slow, lingering, lovely kiss. A soft and warm and sweet kiss that was still sensual enough to get her juices flowing so that when his lips parted, when he took that kiss to the next stage, she was more than willing to part her lips, too.

And, oh, but the jock was a good kisser! That kiss on the cheek the night before really had been a waste of his talents, she thought as he went on giving her a kiss that engulfed her even without his arms around her, that carried her away and made her feel as if she were floating on clouds.

Then he was gone. She opened her eyes, her eyebrows arched in amazement.

"I suppose I shouldn't have done that," Hutch said in a deep, raspy voice that held no remorse that she could distinguish.

Which she was glad of because all Issa wanted was for him to do it again. So rather than agree that he shouldn't have done it, she smiled a coy smile and said, "Yeah, look what happens when the chaperone is off jumping on a trampoline."

Hutch grinned, still remorseless, but after a squeeze of his hands around hers, he let go and put some distance between them.

"It's past that chaperone's bedtime," he said. "Unless you want to stay awhile longer and get in a few more reps," he added facetiously, nodding at the Pec Deck.

Only if each one was followed up with another kiss.

But, of course, she didn't say that. Instead she said, "I think I better give the machine a rest. I wouldn't want to wear it out. How would you ever sell it then?"

"True, true," he played along. "It may never be the same as it is. I might have to mark it half off."

"Sorry about that," Issa mock apologized as she took her arms down and stood.

She hadn't correctly gauged how much space Hutch

had left between himself and the Pec Deck, though, and she suddenly found herself standing close in front of him. Unintentionally. But once she was there, she was there. And neither of them made a move to change that situation. At least not for a moment during which Issa was willing Hutch to kiss her again. A moment during which she thought he might.

But he didn't.

Instead, with a smile that conveyed that he really was tempted, he said, "It's probably better if I *don't* take you up to my office. So why don't you have Ash show you how good he is at bowling while I get the papers I need, and then we can go?"

It was on the tip of Issa's tongue to ask what would happen if he *did* take her up to his office. But she fought the urge. Along with the other urges she was fighting. She merely said, "Okay," before she headed in the direction of the children's section, while Hutch went up a set of stairs that ran along a far wall.

Joining Ash, Issa had only to ask him to show her how to bowl and the two-and-a-half-year-old leaped off the trampoline.

Apparently experienced at how to operate the miniature bowling lane, he pushed a button that caused the whole thing to light up and make sounds like a real bowling alley.

Then, with plastic ball in hand, he showed her his prowess by rolling it into the plastic pins that tipped over and stayed down while a voice announced the count before the pins popped up again a moment later and the ball was returned.

"You're a great bowler!" Issa complimented the toddler, clapping for him as he repositioned himself for another try.

But Issa didn't see that one because, suddenly having the sense she was being watched, she glanced up at the higher level loft that was about half the size of the ground floor.

Sure enough, Hutch was standing at a window that looked out from what must have been his office. Studying her with a serene sort of smile on his handsome face.

Then his glance went to his son and his expression changed.

It made Issa think that something about Ash gave him second thoughts about that kiss Hutch had just given her.

And somehow she knew that regardless of how much she might have wanted to be kissed again—possibly good-night—it wasn't going to happen.

That oh-so-lovely little kiss that had stirred more in her than it should have was the only kiss she was getting tonight.

Chapter Seven

Issa had Friday night to herself. There were any number of things she could have done. Dag and Shannon had invited her to a dinner they were having with friends. But the friends were people she didn't know and her shyness had prompted her to beg off from that.

There was a new release movie at the theater that her old friend Neily Pratt had asked her to see. But part and parcel of that was Issa meeting Neily's husband, Wyatt Grayson, and again, Issa shied away.

She could also have merely gone for a walk in town around the square because there was always something going on there, but that, too, would mean a lot of meeting people and talking.

So—as was most often true of Issa, left to her own devices—she opted for an evening sequestered in her apartment.

The decision for how to spend her time wasn't without its purpose, though. She had a new stack of pamphlets from the obstetrician and a prenatal book the doctor had loaned her. She thought that maybe if she immersed herself in pregnancy literature and made a concerted effort to connect to what she read, the pregnancy might begin to seem real to her. She might begin to feel pregnant.

Then maybe she might be able to fight the insurmountable attraction that was growing for Hutch.

That was her Friday night goal.

Because no pregnant woman should be developing the kind of crush she was developing on a man who wasn't the father of her baby.

No pregnant woman should be allowing a man who wasn't the father of her baby to kiss her the way Hutch had kissed her the previous evening.

And no pregnant woman should be craving more of those kisses—and so much more than mere kisses—the way she was craving that from Hutch.

If she was going to crave something, it should be weird food combinations, not men who had nothing to do with her current situation.

The problem was, she *was* craving more of those kisses from Hutch. And more than that from Hutch. And just about everything else that had to do with Hutch, including and most especially his company.

So she wasn't having much luck even reading the material let alone allowing it to make any impact on her, not when her mind kept wandering to Hutch, to that kiss the night before, to every tiny sound she heard that caused her to listen closely so she could tell if he and Ash were back from the rehearsal dinner for Ian and Jenna's wedding yet.

Pregnant. You're pregnant. Pregnant people don't pine for men who don't have anything to do with their pregnancy, she lectured herself.

But it didn't matter. She still didn't feel pregnant and all she really wanted was to be with Hutch.

So she gave up on the prenatal book and the pamphlets, stuck them in a kitchen drawer and went into her bedroom to make her final decision on what to wear to the wedding tomorrow evening.

The wedding where she and Hutch would both be, but not together, she warned herself as she took out the three dresses that were under consideration.

But just as she did, she heard the distinctive sounds of Hutch coming in downstairs.

She froze.

It was silly, she knew. They didn't have any plans to see each other, so the fact that he was home didn't do anything to alter what she was doing or what she would do for the remainder of the evening.

But somehow just knowing he was in the building, nearby, gave her a tiny rush. Somehow just sitting on the edge of her bed, straining to hear the sounds he made when he ran water, opened and closed a door, sounds she wouldn't have been able to hear if her own place hadn't been dead quiet and if she hadn't been listening, made her happier than she'd been when she'd known he wasn't downstairs.

But still, she wanted to see him.

If only she hadn't already taken out her trash she might be able to do that and run into him in the process.

Maybe she could wad up those pamphlets, put them in a trash bag and take that out.

Then, just as she was plotting, there was a knock on her door.

And in that moment when she just knew it was Hutch outside of her apartment, she thought: *Just go with it. You can't fight it anyway. And it'll resolve itself because ultimately, eventually, you'll feel pregnant, look pregnant and he won't want in on any of it. So enjoy this while you can.*

And as she hurried out of the bedroom to answer her door, she decided that going with the flow of things for now was exactly what she was going to do. Just because she needed a little pleasantness, a little happiness, a little of the calm that Hutch brought with him to get her over the hump.

At the door she paused, belatedly considering what she was wearing—a worn pair of jeans and a plain red T-shirt. And her hair was just pulled up and back into a ponytail at the crown of her head. She had put on mascara, but she suddenly wished she had the time to change clothes, do something else with her hair and add a little more makeup.

Too late, though, she knew. If she took the time to do it now, Hutch would think she was out or asleep or something and leave.

And she wasn't going to risk that.

So she smoothed some stray wisps of hair away from her face and opened the apartment door.

Sure enough, there stood Hutch.

Tall and gorgeous dressed in gray slacks and a white shirt that had a silver-gray cast to it. The collar was open, the sleeves were rolled to his elbows, and in one hand he held a plate with a miniature Bundt cake on it.

"Tunnel-of-Fudge super-chocolate cake," he said by

way of greeting. "It was dessert at the rehearsal dinner and I brought mine home. I thought you might like to share it."

"A man after my own heart," Issa rhapsodized as she pretended to ogle the cake rather than Hutch. Then she looked beyond him for Ash. "You're alone?"

"Ash conked out at the dinner and gave me the excuse to leave so I could get this home to you." He held up his other hand and displayed the baby monitor she hadn't seen until then. "I put him to bed, but my door is open and I could hear him a mile away with this thing. If he so much as rolls over, I'll know it."

"We can leave this door open, too, just in case," Issa said, again thrilled with the thought that Hutch had had her in mind even when he wasn't with her.

"Come in," she invited, stepping out of the way so he could. "Milk, coffee, tea, water?"

"I don't know about you, but I just need a fork," Hutch answered.

Issa went into the kitchen and brought back two forks and two napkins.

"There was a lot of rolling-the-eyes-in-ecstasy over this. Let's see if it's as good as everyone said it was," Hutch suggested.

He put the baby monitor on the end table and together they sat in the center of the sofa—Issa with her legs curled to one side so she could fully face Hutch, and Hutch with one leg curved onto the couch, his other foot on the floor. She held the cake-laden paper plate between them.

"How was the rehearsal and dinner?" Issa asked as they dug into the decadent dessert from opposite ends.

"Okay," he said provisionally. "I wished you were

there about a hundred times, but other than that, it was nice."

He said that so matter-of-factly, as if wishing she were there was nothing. But it wasn't nothing to Issa. She basked in the thought that he'd wanted her with him tonight. Like she'd wanted him with her—against all rhyme or reason.

They agreed that the dense, dark chocolate cake with the fudgy tunnel running through it was, indeed, eye-rolling good. Then Hutch said, "What about you? How was your day and evening?"

"Quiet," she said, having no intention of letting him know her own feelings. "I just stayed in, did some reading, some laundry, you know, not much of anything. This cake is definitely the highlight." The cake and the company.

"Is this the way other men have gotten to your heart—through cake?" he joked.

"Hmm, let's see." She considered that. "Of the grand total of three men that I've had in my life—"

"*Three?* Come on, you've had more guys than that in your life," he cajoled.

"Well, sure, in the whole spectrum of my life, I know more than three men. But men who have gotten to my heart? Nope, only three. Fatally shy, remember?"

"I suppose that doesn't lend itself to a lot of dating," he conceded.

"No, it doesn't. In fact, in high school, I liked the same guy all of sophomore and junior year, but didn't have the courage to speak to him until we were seniors."

Hutch laughed. "That *is* bad. And here? In Northbridge? You'd probably played in the sandbox with the guy."

"He actually didn't move into town until sophomore year, but I can't say it would have been any different even if I had grown up with him. Other than my brothers, boys made me *really* tongue-tied."

"And *was* there cake with High School Boy?"

"Cake and punch. At the school dances we went to. But I only remember that too-sweet white cake with the bad frosting."

"And it *has* to be chocolate to get to your heart," Hutch put in.

"Absolutely. No way to my heart with white cake."

"So that guy was history. What about after high school?"

"I met College Boy sophomore year, too, but sophomore year of college."

"I hope it didn't take you two years to talk to him."

"He asked to borrow my physics notes the second month of school and it went quickly from there because he was *not* shy. None of the three were—I'm convinced that that was part of the draw. It's always been an opposites-attract thing for me when it comes to who I've gotten involved with."

"Ah, but was there cake?" Hutch said, keeping with the game so the tone remained light.

"College Boy liked chocolate as much as I do. So yes, there was cake whenever we could get it. Chocolate cake, chocolate candy, chocolate cookies, brownies, fudge—you name it. But his personality was bigger-than-life and so was his appetite."

"Was he a sumo wrestler?"

Issa laughed. "He was thin as a rail but ate like a

fiend. And I can't say that he endeared himself to me by always eating the last of *my* dessert when he finished his own—because that's what he did, *every* time," she said as if it had been a crime.

Hutch grinned and handed over the plate. There was only one bite of cake left. "Here, you can have that. I don't want demerits."

Issa laughed, but the cake was too good to refuse the last bite. "I can't be a martyr," she announced just before devouring it, making Hutch grin in response.

"What happened to High School Boy and College Boy?" Hutch asked then.

"Nothing dramatic. High school ended, I graduated from college, and my experience with the gregarious, unreserved, have-a-good-time guys is that they don't take things too seriously. I saw in advance that the relationships weren't going anywhere, so I wasn't too invested. I parted ways amiably with both guys. I still hear from College Boy through emails every now and then."

"And after college?"

That sobered her. "David."

"Third, of three."

Issa knew what Hutch was thinking. And he was right, so she didn't deny it. "David is the irresponsible responsible party," she said, alluding to her pregnancy as she set the paper plate, forks and napkins on the coffee table. "There was chocolate cake with David as long as I bought it. So you probably couldn't say that his way to my heart was through cake, but maybe my way to his was." And her tone was certainly not as frivolous as it had been in telling about the other two men she'd dated.

"You don't have to talk about him if you don't want to. But I'd like to know."

She didn't believe that Hutch had come tonight with the goal of getting her to talk about her romantic history. Of course he was curious about the father of her baby—she knew that everyone would be. But she was so glad he'd thought of her throughout the rehearsal and dinner, so glad he was there with her, that she opted to fill him in on what she'd avoided telling him before.

"I worked with David's sister," she said. "Deana was the secretary at the school where I taught. She brought him to the faculty Christmas party three years ago and introduced us. I'd had wine, so I was more relaxed than usual. And David was my kind of guy—friendly, charismatic, talkative, extroverted. Exactly like his two predecessors and the opposite of me."

"Hey! There is nothing wrong with my quiet tenant and I'm not letting you say anything against her. I happen to think pretty highly of her."

Issa laughed in embarrassment even though it was particularly nice to hear him say that.

"Still," she insisted, "David was the life of any party. Just like my high school sweetheart and the guy I was with in college. Which made it easy for me to hang back—and maybe that was part of my appeal."

"That you hung back?" Hutch asked with a perplexed expression.

"I didn't get in the way of their being the life of the party, I didn't want to share the spotlight, and I think that might have been behind their attraction to me."

"That and the fact that you're beautiful and sweet and—"

Issa felt her cheeks heat. She couldn't let him go

on even though she was once more happy to know he thought those things about her.

"Anyway," she said to interrupt him, "David in particular was... Well, if he was in a room, *everyone* else paled by comparison. He told jokes and stories like a stand-up comedian, he remembered everyone's name and even small details about them that he would seem genuinely interested in talking about—and he could talk about anything. He was a charmer. Next to that, I could be invisible, which is kind of the way I like it."

"So men have been the beard that hid your proverbial weak chin, is that what you're telling me?" Hutch teased with a gentle smile.

"That's what I'm telling you. And in the meantime, I had companionship, a date, someone to do things with," she admitted.

"Okay, so men have been your beard. But with this David, it was you who had to buy the cake?" Hutch asked.

"David is one of those guys who everyone likes so much that they excuse his faults."

"His faults being?"

"He's a wannabe musician who can't support himself. That means he makes a little money when his friends hire him to play at their weddings or parties, or when someone has him give their kids piano lessons for a while. But other than that—"

"How does he live?"

"Off family, friends. He lived off of me," she confessed reluctantly, quietly. "He *pretends* that he wants to work, that he's looking for a job, that it's just bad luck that he never gets one. But everyone loves him, so someone else always picks up the check for David.

Or buys him drinks, or lets him use their car or borrow their clothes if he has a gig. Someone is always willing to let him crash at their place."

"He didn't live with you?"

"He did. But before that and whenever we'd break up—"

"Was there a lot of that?"

"There was," Issa admitted. "Every time I put any pressure on him to act like an adult, to get a real job, to take some responsibility, he would say he didn't need me nagging him and he would walk out. That's when he'd end up on a friend's couch or in their guest room again—the way he lived between relationships."

"But you'd get back together?" Hutch asked.

"I told you, David can charm the bark off of a tree," Issa said. "And every time he'd come back, he would either have job prospects or he'd actually have a job, so I'd hope things were turning around."

"But they weren't?"

"The prospects never panned out, and even if he had a job, he wouldn't keep it for longer than a month after I let him come back." Issa shrugged and confessed, "I cared for David. I kept hoping he'd get himself together, grow up, actually do what he promised he was going to do—for his sake as much as for mine and for the sake of our relationship."

"But he didn't."

She shook her head. "No, he didn't. And then I sold Gob-o-Goo."

"Which was good, wasn't it?" Hutch prompted, probably because her tone had been so dire.

"It was good. But by then I was getting fed up with David, I was coming to grips with the fact that he wasn't ever likely to get himself together, to do anything more than he had been doing. And about the time I was thinking that, Gob-o-Goo went into production and I overheard him tell one of his friends that he'd struck gold, that he never had to worry about working again, that he'd just keep me inventing things and stay on that gravy train."

Hutch's brows drew together angrily. "Oh, boy, that guy needed some sense knocked into him."

Issa didn't refute that sentiment. "That was six months ago and, like I said, I was pretty fed up even before that. But hearing him say what he said was the straw that broke the camel's back. I could see that I was more a meal ticket for him than anything and I ended it with him."

"Good for you," Hutch encouraged.

He hesitated and Issa could tell that something else was on his mind. Then he said, "But you're two months pregnant."

Issa was just waiting for that. "Yeah, not a part of the story I'm proud of," she admitted sheepishly.

"You had a moment of weakness."

There was so much acceptance in that that it made it easier for Issa to tell him the rest. "David moved out, but he moved out to a series of couches and guest rooms until he could find someone who would let him share an apartment in trade for cleaning and taking out the trash—that was his plan."

"He didn't have any intention of paying his own way even then?"

"No. And until he could find that kind of arrangement or a place to store what few belongings he had that didn't fit into a suitcase, I still had some of his stuff.

But he finally made a deal with someone and came back to get it."

"Uh-oh."

Issa nodded. "Work and home, work and home—that's all I did. Pretty much all I'd been doing for the four months he'd been gone. The few friends I had in Seattle were married. I didn't have any family there. And given the choice between going out by myself or staying in—"

"You stayed in. But that doesn't mean you didn't get lonely," Hutch said for her.

"And David showed up with a bottle of wine as thanks for having kept his things for four months. He opened the wine and poured on the charm and I had one stupid, weak moment, and…" Issa sighed in resignation. "Well, add a birth control malfunction to it and here I am."

She couldn't look Hutch in the eye, so she glanced downward and began to fiddle with a loose string on the pocket of her jeans.

"Does he know?" Hutch asked softly.

"Oh, he knows," Issa said with some acrimony. "All it took was the sun coming up the next morning for me to realize I'd made a mistake and I told him so. He was angry—I think he really thought that he was going to get back on the gravy train. We didn't part on good terms. Then I found out I was pregnant. I thought he had a right to know, so I called him." Again Issa shook her head, recalling that conversation.

"It didn't go well," Hutch guessed.

"David was still David. At first he tried to use it as a way to get back in with me, so I could support him. I said no, that what was between us was over, but that if he wanted to be involved with the child—"

"I can't see that," Hutch muttered.

"It did just make him mad again. He doesn't even want to be responsible for himself, let alone for anyone else. Anyway, when I said no to getting back together with him for the sake of the baby, he went to the other extreme and demanded that I end the pregnancy."

"But that wasn't what you wanted, either."

"I'd already decided against that before I ever told David. I came from a big family and..." Another shrug. "I don't know... Even though I'm not really mother material, it seemed as if this baby was there for a reason. And I *wanted* to have it, although I'm not sure I can explain that phenomenon because I'm also freaked out about it."

"How did he react to the news that you wouldn't end the pregnancy?"

"He hit the ceiling. He said that even if I did go through with it I better not expect him to have any part of it, that he wasn't supporting a kid."

"No surprise there," Hutch said under his breath, disgusted.

"Right," Issa agreed. "But by then, I really, really knew there was nothing between us, I'd already made up my mind to do the whole thing on my own, so it wasn't a surprise or a blow. But David was crashing with a friend of his who's a lawyer and the lawyer advised him to get everything in writing. There were legal papers drawn up— David relinquished all paternal rights, and I swore that I wouldn't ever go after him for child support. And that was it."

"That was the loose end in Seattle that was tied up

good and tight, and why it was so over that it was better to leave Seattle in the dust, wasn't it?"

He was repeating what she'd told him Tuesday night. "There are definitely no loose ends there now," she confirmed.

"So you came back to Northbridge," Hutch finished for her.

"I'd actually decided to do that before I became pregnant—right after I made David move out. I wanted to be back here, near family, even though I'm not always good at socializing with them, either," she said quietly, thinking about the dinner with Dag and Shannon that she'd turned down because she knew it wouldn't have been dinner with only Dag and Shannon.

"But I'm sure being pregnant made it all the more important to at least be in the proximity of family," Hutch said, once more understanding.

"For sure."

"And yet you still haven't told anyone?"

She shook her head. "I know they'll be supportive and help and do whatever I need them to. It's just so embarrassing that it happened and that the man it happened with was such a jerk."

"Hey, we're all just human," Hutch assured her in that comforting way he had that actually made her feel less embarrassed.

In fact, it made her comfortable enough to stop fiddling with the loose string and glance up at his handsome face again.

"You know…" he said, "if it would help, I'd go with you to tell your family."

Issa appreciated the offer but it just made her smile. "Thanks, I wish I could take you up on that. But this is probably something I should do alone. When I get up the courage."

Hutch nodded. "Well, if you change your mind…"

"I can just picture it," Issa said, laughing at the image she had of that scenario. "The first thing the family would think was that because you were there, you were the father."

"We just met. All they'd have to do is the math."

"Sure, but if you were with me to tell them, their initial thought would be that you were in on it."

He grinned. "The shotguns would come out and I'd be sunk?"

She laughed again, lightening the tone. "You never know," she played along.

"Still, I'd take my chances. When the time comes, if you want the moral support, just let me know."

Which was more than the actual father of the baby was willing to do, Issa thought, appreciating the difference between the two men.

Hutch stretched an arm along the top of the sofa back and traced her cheek with the knuckle of his index finger, smiling a kind smile. "So you do want this baby. Tonight is the first time you've said that."

"Yeah. It's just one of the many things that are hard for me to believe—that I really am pregnant and will have a kid and be a parent." She shrugged once more. "It's all tough to grasp right now, but it's true."

Hutch nodded. "It's kind of hard for me to believe you're pregnant, too," he seemed to confess. "I can't say that the two things have come together in my mind— you and pregnant. There's really just you in here," he said, tapping his temple with his index finger.

"Well, because it hasn't come together in my mind,

it's no wonder it hasn't come together in yours. So don't feel bad. I'm just hoping that I won't totally mess up the whole parenthood thing."

"That's where I come in, and we're working on it, remember? And look at it like this, if you're lucky you'll have a kid who thinks you're as fantastic as Ash thinks you are."

Issa laughed. "Ash thinks I'm fantastic?"

"He does. I had to buy my son a girl's doll this morning because of you."

"You did?" Issa asked.

"We went into the toy store so I could get him something that might keep him occupied through tonight's rehearsal and tomorrow night's wedding. But all he wanted was an *Itta doll*—a blond curvy little number that he apparently thinks is your replica."

"No!" Issa said with a laugh.

"Oh, yeah. My son is now carrying around a doll that he thinks is you. A doll that he thinks is great because he thinks that you're great."

Issa couldn't help laughing again, but Hutch didn't seem to take offense. He was smiling, too. And looking at her very intently.

Then, in a quieter voice, he said, "And how can I disagree with the boy when he's right—you *are* great."

"Don't forget that I ate the last bite of cake. That's not so great," Issa joked because while she was once more pleased by what he'd said, she was also once more embarrassed by it and didn't know how to respond.

"Okay, one flaw," he conceded. "Remind me to hold it against you."

"Ah, reminding you of my flaws is *not* my responsibility," she countered, making him grin.

But as he went on looking into her eyes, the grin changed to a more thoughtful smile. A more intimate smile to go along with his continuing to smooth her cheek with his knuckle for a moment more before he slipped his hand to her nape.

Still holding her eyes with his, he did a slight massage that wiped away the tension put there by talking about her past. And unlike the night before when he'd taken her by surprise by kissing her on the Pec Deck, tonight she knew it was coming because he moved nearer at a slow but steady rate.

She could have drawn back and made sure it didn't happen.

But she'd already decided she was going to go with the flow, that whatever it was that had sparked between them would find its own resolution, so she might as well enjoy it while it lasted.

So she leaned the slightest fraction of an inch forward. And when his lips met hers, she let her eyes drift closed and sailed right into the kiss, which began the way the kiss the night before had ended—soft and warm and sweet with that underlying sensuality.

The sensuality wasn't so muted tonight, though. His lips parted wider over hers, and urged hers to part wider, too. His tongue was tentative at first, toying with her, inviting hers to play.

And oooh, but he was good at it when she accepted the invitation, when he took that exceptional kiss from last night and made it even better. Much better.

Slow and languorous, enticing and teasing, stealthy and playful by turns, Issa followed his lead and made a few contributions of her own that provoked him to deepen the kiss even more, to wrap his free arm around her and pull her closer.

She'd itched to press her palms to his pectorals Thursday night when she'd watched them flex on the exercise machine. She'd itched to know if they were as rock-solid as they looked. And when he brought her nearer, that was where her hands went without even thinking about it, reflexively, realizing only once they got there that she was getting what she'd wanted the previous night.

As good as his chest looked, it felt even better. It was definitely a hard wall of divine muscle beneath her palms.

His hand cradled her at her nape as the kiss intensified. Their mouths opened wider and his tongue nearly ravaged hers as sensual went all the way to sexy.

He kissed her until she was breathless and yet she just wanted him to go on kissing her, never to stop.

She slid her hands from his chest up the thickness of his neck to his coarse hair as their heads swayed and their tongues did a diabolically delicious dance. She felt her nipples harden to diamonds. She ached for their chests to touch but they just weren't close enough.

But then, just as Issa was getting so lost in that kiss, in what her body was beginning to want, Hutch toned things down. Little by little his tongue bid hers a fond, reluctant farewell. Little by little there was reversal and retreat, until a few chaste, parting kisses finally took his mouth away once and for all.

Issa drew her hands from him, but Hutch didn't let go of her. He sat up straighter, pulled her forehead to his chest and then dropped his chin to her crown.

"Tomorrow is the wedding," he said in a voice too

raspy for her to have any doubts that the kiss had been as powerful for him as it had been for her, even if he had been the one to end it. "I have to be up at dawn and running around all day. I should get out of here."

Except that he didn't move, other than to bring his face into her hair and kiss the top of her head. Then he said, "I'll have to meet you there, but will you be my date for the shindig afterward?"

"The reception?" Issa asked with a small chuckle at his terminology.

"Yeah, that," he said as if his mind were too foggy from their kiss to have found the right word himself. "I told you, I spent the whole time at the rehearsal and dinner wishing I was there with you. I knew then that I wanted to make sure I could be with you tomorrow night."

Issa smiled even though he couldn't see it. Or maybe more so because he couldn't see it.

"Or do you have other plans?" he asked when she was too busy smiling to answer him.

"I was going with Dag and Shannon and then we're set to meet up with the rest of the family there," she said.

"So how about if you go with Dag and Shannon, then we can meet up after the ceremony and I'll take you home? Ash and I will both be in tuxes, if that helps persuade you. And I don't know about mine, but he looks sharp in his."

Yet again he made Issa laugh. "I've heard that you can never turn down a man in a tux," she said facetiously.

"Then you'll be my date?"

"I don't know if we should call it that."

"You'll help me wrangle Ash and, in the process, get some experience with kids," he amended, putting it in terms of the more acceptable arrangement they'd made at the start.

"Okay," Issa said, not really having had any inclination to deny herself his company at the wedding even though she probably should.

He kissed her head again, his breath warm against her scalp, before he did finally let go of her. He got to his feet and snatched the baby monitor from the end table as she sat up straight and watched him.

"Do *not* walk me to the door," he said when she made a move to stand. "Saying good-night there is only going to get me into more trouble."

Did that mean that he would kiss her again if she went to the door with him?

Ah, the temptation.

But she stayed where she was and merely followed him with her eyes as he crossed to the apartment door.

"I'll see you tomorrow night. You'll recognize me. I'll be the one with the son carrying a doll."

Issa grinned at that. "I'll be there," she assured him.

Then he waved, went out into the hallway and pulled her apartment door closed between them.

And that was when Issa deflated right there on the couch.

In what she thought might very well qualify as a belated swoon.

A swoon from that kiss that she had every intention of taking to bed with her to relive again and again.

Chapter Eight

"What's that boy doing with a doll?" Morgan Kincaid blustered as he entered the church basement Saturday evening.

The male members of the wedding party were gathered in a room to dress just before the ceremony that would marry Ian Kincaid and Jenna Bowen. Already in his own tuxedo, Hutch and Ian's father announced his arrival with that bit of criticism. Apparently Ash and Ash's new favorite possession were the first things the elder Kincaid saw when he entered the room.

"Leave him alone, Dad," Hutch warned. "He picked it, he likes it, it's his. He thinks it's a toy version of our tenant—Issa McKendrick—and I'm pretty sure he's got a little thing for her."

Put in those terms the idea made Morgan Kincaid chuckle. "The boy's got good taste. Somebody just introduced me to her on my way in. She could be a blond bombshell if she just opened her mouth and talked once in a while."

"Actually, I'd say that Issa is more the classic blond beauty than the blond bombshell. And she opens her mouth and talks just fine once you get to know her. She just tends to be a little bashful and that makes her quiet around new people," Hutch explained, correcting his father's assessment of Issa.

"Is that so?" Morgan Kincaid said. "Maybe you should have bought yourself a doll, too. Sounds like the boy isn't the only one of you to have a little *thing* for her."

"Or maybe Hutch doesn't need the toy version," Ian goaded in true brotherly spirit but less annoyingly. "Maybe Hutch has the real deal. Even though that house of his is set up as two apartments, he and Issa *are* under one roof."

"Issa and I are getting acquainted," Hutch said as he and Ian went to stand in front of the mirrors that had been set up for their use. "We're friendly. Friends—I guess you could say we're becoming friends." He made that amendment because *friendly* sounded like more than friends somehow.

Of course, kissing like they'd been kissing wasn't what friends did, but he wasn't going to tell anyone about that. Especially because he couldn't quite condone it himself.

He just seemed helpless when it came to resisting the urge.

But again, that was not something he was going to tell his father or his brother.

"Gettin' back in the game, are you, Hutch?" his father said. "Well, remember that we Kincaids are trying to build a good name for ourselves in this town. That's important with the Monarchs' training center coming here. I wouldn't want us associated with any heartbreaking. It could make us look bad."

"Don't worry, my player days are behind me all the way around," Hutch assured his father with some impatience.

"I should hope so," Morgan Kincaid said before moving off to have his boutonniere put on for him as Hutch and Ian worked with their own cummerbunds.

"Some things never change," Hutch muttered once the older man was out of earshot.

"You know how he is," Ian said.

"Only too well."

"But *are* you starting something up with Issa McKendrick?"

"Are you worried, too?" Hutch countered with another question rather than answering the one his brother had asked.

"Not worried. Just interested," Ian said.

It wasn't easy reconciling a six-year long rift in the family, but Hutch knew that Ian was putting real effort into repairing their relationship as brothers. It was something Hutch wanted, too, so he curbed the aggravation their father had just caused him and stopped looking for ulterior motives in Ian.

"I like Issa, but it isn't going anywhere. And not because I'm afraid of making the Kincaids look bad. These days I have my own reasons for keeping to the straight and narrow."

Which was true. Even if those reasons were hard to remember when he was alone with Issa, when he was enjoying being with her, when he looked into those incredible sapphire-blue eyes of hers and all he could think about was how much he wanted her.

"Your own reasons," Ian repeated. "Too soon after Iris?" he asked with some concern.

Actually, for the first time, Iris wasn't a factor, which was part of why his attraction to Issa was flourishing. In the year and a half since Iris's death, Hutch had been set up on a few dates and there had even been one woman he'd invited to dinner on his own. But each time it was as if, in his mind's eye, Iris was sitting beside his date, right there for comparison. And no one had lived up to his late wife.

But with Issa it was different.

He wasn't even inclined to compare her to Iris. Somehow she was her own entirely new entity. With Issa, all he thought about was Issa.

And that was nice. It didn't leave him feeling as if he were trying—and failing—to recapture something he'd lost. It felt fresh. And good. Like getting a second wind.

Or a second chance.

But he couldn't think of it like that. That was going too far.

"No, it isn't about Iris," he answered his brother as they both tied their bow ties. But Ash *was* an issue and to remind himself of that, he said, "When it comes to Ash, though, I have to be careful. He has to be my number one priority and I can't let anything or anyone distract me from him."

"Sure, that makes sense," Ian agreed. "But you have to have a life, too. You can't *just* be a dad."

"I have to be a dad first. Ash's dad."

He stopped himself short, before he gave away the

secret that when it came to Issa, there would soon be another child for someone to be a dad to.

But even though he didn't say it, even though it was something he consistently lost sight of, his silence and the lack of reality it had for him didn't change the fact that Issa *was* pregnant. And that was a complication. Her baby was something, someone, who could be another distraction from Ash if Hutch ended up being around when that child came.

And there were other Ash issues, too.

"I also can't bring in just anyone to be Ash's stepmother," Hutch said as he and Ian each began to put gold links into the cuffs of their tuxedo shirts. "I don't know if you know anything about the McKendricks, but Issa told me what a lousy stepmother her mother was to Logan and Hadley. I wouldn't let anything like that happen to Ash."

"Sure, but Issa isn't her mother," Ian reasoned.

"Still," Hutch said, unsure yet what kind of stepmother Issa might make. "Plus there's attachment issues with Ash," he added then, again more for his own benefit than to reveal anything to his brother. "I don't want Ash getting attached to someone only to have that someone flake out on him."

Ian nodded in the direction of the little boy, who seemed to be making his Issa doll fly like a superhero. "Are you sure he isn't already attached?"

"Nah. He likes Issa—that's why he wanted the doll. But he isn't depending on her for anything. She doesn't have any place in his routine. She's just the pretty lady who lives upstairs and hangs out with us now and then."

Without interfering with anything, and without even being a distraction from Ash, Hutch admitted to himself. He and Issa had made Ash a priority—Ash was even getting extra attention from her parenting practice. Or like last night, Hutch saw Issa after his son was asleep, taking nothing away from the two-and-a-half-year-old.

There wasn't any harm in any of that, he realized.

And that thought stuck with him.

If spending time with Issa the way he and Ash had been wasn't doing harm, then why did he keep beating himself up for it?

Lately, he seemed to always be seesawing between wanting to see Issa every minute that he could, and feeling guilty for how much he wanted to see her. And then guilty for things like kissing her. But maybe it wasn't such a big deal.

Their original agreement was in force—she was gaining some skills, some experience, some confidence in dealing with a kid.

And through Issa, he was getting to know more about living in Northbridge, about the town itself and the people and how things worked.

If, along with those needs being met, he was also getting the pleasure of Issa's company—the valued company of another adult, who proved to him that he actually could move past his grief and loss to enjoy being with a woman again—what was so wrong with that?

Ian was right. He couldn't be *just* a dad. He did need a little bit of a life for himself, didn't he?

No harm, no foul.

So maybe he could just take it for what it was and enjoy it.

"Well, Issa *is* a pretty lady," Ian said, breaking into

Hutch's thoughts. "Dad's right. The kid does have good taste."

"Yep," Hutch agreed.

And now that he'd given himself permission to do some coasting on what was happening with Issa rather than trying to fight it?

He couldn't wait for this wedding to get going so the reception would start and he could be with her again.

"What good is it to have a daughter if you can't get her to dance with you?" Morgan Kincaid demanded.

What good is it to have a daughter? Issa cringed a little at the older man's words to Lacey Kincaid, Hutch and Ian's younger sister.

"Nice invitation, Dad," Lacey said, apparently of the same mind as Issa. "I'm worthless to you in any other way?"

"Oh, don't get all prickly," the former football great reprimanded. "I was just kidding."

To Issa and Hutch, Lacey said, "He believes that, too."

Then Hutch's extremely pretty sister sighed and got up from the table she'd shared with Issa, Hutch, Ash and Morgan Kincaid throughout the reception, and said, "Okay, Dad, let's dance."

"Hey," Hutch said to stall them. "I need to get Ash home, so we're probably going to say good-night and take off. I'll talk to you before you leave tomorrow, Lace. And Dad, because you're leaving Northbridge to-night, I'll probably see you when you're in town next."

"Maybe you can get a football instead of a doll into that boy's hands by then," the older man answered with what was apparently intended as a goodbye.

"It was nice meeting you, Issa," Lacey said after another roll of her eyes at her father. "I imagine that with both of my brothers in Northbridge, I'll be back. Maybe we can have lunch or dinner?"

"I'd like that," Issa said, meaning it because Lacey was so nice and so friendly that she'd made it easy for Issa to get past her usual reticence and relax.

At least she'd relaxed with Lacey. Issa had continued to find Morgan Kincaid daunting and hadn't said much to him at all.

But apparently his daughter's good manners reminded him to show some himself and he said a curt "Pleasure" to convey his perfunctory sentiments.

"Good to meet you, too, Mr. Kincaid...Morgan," Issa amended in a hurry because he'd told her at least three times to use his first name. It just didn't seem appropriate when he was as imposing as he was.

Then Morgan Kincaid led his daughter onto the dance floor and Hutch said, "Do you mind leaving? I probably should have asked before I made the announcement, but I thought you might be about ready to put an evening with my father behind you, too."

"It's fine with me," Issa said, sidestepping his comment about Morgan Kincaid. "I've talked to everyone I know and Ash is worn-out," she added, motioning toward the two-and-a-half-year-old who had crawled into her lap to help eat her slice of wedding cake and then collapsed there half awake, half asleep. He was still clutching the doll that so irked his grandfather.

"Let's go before the dance ends, then," Hutch said, getting up to take his son from Issa.

Ash didn't protest the way he had when Morgan Kincaid had tried to get the toddler to leave Issa's lap and go to him. Ash went to his father willingly, dropping his head to one of Hutch's broad shoulders the minute Hutch picked him up.

"Don't forget our chocolate boxes," he advised, nodding toward the favor that adorned each place setting—a small square box made of milk chocolate and decorated with dark chocolate and baby-blue fondant flowers—Jenna's colors. Inside the box were three chocolate truffles that had been the talk of the reception.

Issa picked up hers, Hutch's and Ash's by the ribbon wrapped around them for transport. That way the heat of hands wouldn't melt the chocolate.

On the way out they stopped to once again congratulate Ian and Jenna and say good-night. Issa told Jenna what a beautiful wedding it had been.

And it *had* been a beautiful wedding. The candlelit church had been adorned in bluebell flowers and white baby's breath. The bride's gown was a simple strapless empire waist A-line with a beaded bodice. The bridesmaids had all worn a similar style of dress—strapless empire waists with their bodices a criss-cross of pleated satin rather than beads and their hemlines ending at the knee. There had been four bridesmaids—two in baby-blue satin, two in chocolate-brown. The flower girls—Tia McKendrick and Jenna's adopted daughter, Abby—had worn high-wasted polka dot dresses in those same colors. And because Abby was still too young and unsteady on her feet to walk down the aisle, Tia had pushed her in a small wicker stroller also adorned with flowers and ribbons in blue and brown.

After exchanging those parting pleasantries, Issa took one last look at the candle and flower-strewn church basement, at the blue-and-brown linen-covered tables, and at what remained of the four-tier cake that had a cascade of fondant flowers also in blue and brown, and she and Hutch left.

"Nice wedding," Issa commented on their way to Hutch's SUV.

"It was. And a lot more traditional than mine. Probably what Ian would have had with Iris, too, if they'd gotten to the altar."

Ian and Hutch's late wife? What did that mean?

As Hutch put Ash into the car seat and Issa got into the passenger's side, she wondered if that comment opened the door to her to ask some questions.

Certainly she was curious—much more about his late wife than whatever kind of wedding they'd had. But now, with that other remark about his late wife and his brother, her curiosity was at a new high. It was just difficult to know if it was a subject she could delve into.

He *had* said it himself, though.

Before she had the chance to broach it, Hutch got behind the wheel, started the engine and said, "I was thinking tonight would be a chance for you to get some experience putting a mostly asleep kid to bed."

"How hard can it be? He's mostly asleep," Issa said, willing to lengthen her time with Hutch in whatever way she could but sorry that they'd moved on to a different subject.

"Ah, but the point is to keep him mostly asleep."

"Maybe you shouldn't trust me with it, then."

He smiled over at her. "You'll do fine. I'll whisper you through it."

Which was exactly what he did when they reached

home. Hutch whispered his instructions for how to gingerly undress Ash and get him into his pajamas.

"Don't tell his dentist, but we skip the toothbrushing on nights like this," he confided as he had her lift Ash carefully into his bed and tuck him in.

She almost caused a disaster when she forgot his doll and gave him only his floppy lion, Za-Za. Ash woke enough to groggily complain and demand it, but it seemed to help that she was there to give it to him. She even indulged a surprising inclination to kiss the child's forehead and smooth back his hair when he was settled against his pillow with his doll and lion beside him, before she relinquished the bedside spot to Hutch to do much the same.

Then she and Hutch quietly left Ash's room and went into the living room.

"Perfect!" Hutch praised at a normal octave again once they were there. "Now we can enjoy our chocolate boxes and share Ash's, too!"

Issa laughed. "This whole thing was just so we could steal candy from a baby?"

"I heard the fresh peach-mango truffle was so good it would make you cry. So, yes."

Issa laughed at him. But because she welcomed any excuse to keep the evening going a while longer, she merely let him lead her to the sofa.

Issa was wearing a slinky knit dress that fit her top half like a second skin and then flared into a full skirt that reached her calves. What dressed it up was the filmy shrug that went over it. Adorned with sequined flowers, the shrug tied just below her breasts in a sheer veil that allowed the spaghetti straps of her dress to show through and framed the dress's V neckline with its own open-front edges.

The fullness of the skirt let Issa sit at an angle on the couch, facing the center in anticipation of where Hutch would end up once he'd discarded his tuxedo jacket, bow tie and cummerbund. Issa tried not to make it obvious that she was watching. But she enjoyed the sight.

She even thought it was sexy when he removed his cufflinks and rolled his sleeves to mid-forearm, but she did her best to hide what was going through her mind.

Once he'd joined her on the sofa, he reached over to the coffee table and retrieved two of the three chocolate boxes, setting one in Issa's lap and keeping the other for himself. "I don't think it matters which one came from which place setting, does it?" he asked.

"I hope not because I didn't keep track," Issa answered as they both untied the ribbons from around their respective boxes.

But when Issa peered into hers, she said, "Uh-oh, looks like it does matter. This one must have come from Ash's place setting because it's filled with jelly beans."

"Ah, and here I thought we were gonna score some extra truffles. Too bad," Hutch lamented, taking the box from Issa and exchanging it for the other one on the coffee table.

That one did, indeed, have truffles in it, and after agreeing that they really were to-die-for, Issa opted for eating only one, along with a chunk of chocolate she broke off the box's lid before putting it back on the table.

Then she decided to test the waters to see if she could return to that intriguing comment Hutch had made when they'd left the church. "So what *was* your wedding like?" she ventured.

Hutch smiled as he polished off his second truffle. "It was Iris and me in one of those little chapels in Vegas. No fanfare, just a guy with a bad comb-over who performed the ceremony and his wife to witness it."

"And that was it? No family? No friends? No reception or party or anything?"

"That was it. We were in Las Vegas when the football season ended. We'd been talking about getting married and because neither of our families were speaking to us—"

"I'm getting an image that you might want to clear up. There could have been a wedding between Ian and your late wife, neither of your families were speaking to you when you married her... Did you steal your brother's girlfriend or something?"

"Nah, I'd never do that." After his second truffle he set his own chocolate box on the coffee table, too. "But Iris *had* been engaged to Ian at one point. It's kind of convoluted and makes for a long story."

"I don't have any pressing appointments," Issa said to encourage him.

He stretched an arm along the sofa back and settled in. "Okay, you asked for it."

"Gimme all ya got," she joked.

His grin in response to that was full of the devil but he avoided a witty comeback and instead said, "Let's see... How can I put as much of this as possible in a nutshell? I graduated from college, my father negotiated a quarterback spot for me with the South Dakota Stingers which was owned by Dwayne Stinson. Dwayne was the much-older brother of Iris, whom he'd basically raised—"

"And that was how you met."

"That was how we all met each other. The beginning of what my father hoped would lead to his becoming a partner in the Stingers because they were in financial trouble. Owning a team of his own was always his goal."

"You were his foot in the door?"

"I was his *first* foot in the door. Then Ian got together with Iris and ultimately they became engaged, and my father thought that was his second way in."

"Ian got together with Iris," Issa repeated. "But did you have secret feelings for her?"

"Nooo. I knew her. I liked her well enough, but she was just my boss's sister, my brother's girlfriend. I was more interested in my own…pursuits."

"Drinking, partying, playing around." Issa reiterated what he'd told her days before.

"Drinking, partying, playing around," he confirmed.

"But Iris and Ian didn't end up getting married?" Issa asked.

"Nope. About seven or eight months before my contract with Dwayne would expire, Iris broke off her engagement with Ian."

"Why?"

"Well—again the condensed version—Iris had been kind of scattered about figuring out what to do with herself in school and in picking a career. She hadn't stuck to anything. Then she decided she wanted to work in the business end of football, specifically with the Stingers. Dwayne said no."

"To his own sister working in the family business?"

"Family or not, he didn't believe that she would stick with that any more than she'd stuck with anything else. And financially the Stingers were still struggling. He wasn't willing to stretch any of his already-overstretched resources putting her to work, only to have her quit when she broke a nail."

Issa flinched at that. "Is that actually what he told her?"

"It is. Iris tried to get Ian to go to bat for her with her brother, to help convince him that he should take her seriously. But Ian went the other direction—he thought Dwayne was right."

"He sided with her brother rather than with her?" Issa asked in amazement.

"And she broke up with him."

"Is this where you came in?"

"No, not right away, at least. Iris made herself scarce after that. I didn't even see her around. Then, one day, on the verge of my signing a new contract that my father was pushing for—that again was more to Dwayne's advantage than to mine because my father was still hoping Dwayne would let him buy into the team even though that hadn't happened in the three years I'd been playing for the Stingers—Iris showed up on my doorstep."

"Cold and wet and hungry?"

Hutch laughed. "Hardly. She was gunning for bear. She made a business pitch to me that I couldn't believe and she said if I would let her represent me she'd get me what I deserved, whether it was from the Stingers or from someone else."

"Let me guess, you *didn't* side with her brother."

"She was impressive," Hutch said with some residual

awe in his tone. "And I'll admit it was a little galling to have my old man use me on a gambit that wasn't working out for him, that was really only benefiting Dwayne and keeping my father on the hook. I wasn't eager to take on a second round of being paid less than I should have been for that. So, yeah, I signed on with Iris and she became my agent."

"That couldn't have gone over well with *anyone*."

"Nope," Hutch said simply. "My father and her brother were both raging mad. Ian didn't like it, either, but things really hit the fan with him a little later, when Iris and I got personally involved."

"That didn't happen right away?" Issa asked.

"Not right away, no. At first things between Iris and me were strictly business. But she was something to see when she was in action," he said admiringly. "By the time she'd gotten me the sweetest deal in the NFL—with a different team—I'd noticed her in a whole new light."

"And that was when things with Ian went sour?"

Hutch took a deep breath, for the first time sounding as if he had some regrets. "Yeah. Ian was still taking heat from Dad about blowing things with Iris and costing Dad that avenue into Stingers ownership—so Ian wasn't in the best mood. He also thought it was disloyal of me to start anything up with his former fiancée even if a lot of time *had* passed and they'd both moved on. Bottom line—*everybody* was angry, and Iris and I were on our own."

"Which was why only Comb-Over Minister and his wife were at your wedding."

"Exactly."

"And that was okay with you both?" Issa asked.

Hutch shrugged. "It wasn't how we would have liked things to be, but the only other option for us both at the time was to go on doing what other people wanted us to do rather than what was best for us."

"And the family feud lasted how long?"

"About six years—until Shannon and Dag's wedding in March."

"It wasn't even resolved when Ash was born?" Issa asked.

Hutch shook his head. "Nope. Iris was hoping that might help—with her brother, at least—so she sent him a birth announcement. He sent it back. We got the message—we were still pariahs, so I didn't even make any attempt with my family. We just went about our own business."

"Starting the stores?"

"Actually, the first store had opened right about the time Iris got pregnant. When she decided she wanted to start a family, she also got more worried about the potential for injury if I went on playing football. And I wasn't interested in being the absentee father my father was through every training camp and football season. So she came up with the idea of the sporting goods store."

"I take it that didn't get any notice from the families, either."

"Nah. Although I almost expected a rise out of my father over using the Kincaid name. But he ignored it."

"And also didn't make any overtures."

Hutch shrugged. "You know how fights are—once they get started, once no one is speaking, it's tough to end it."

"But you and Iris were happy together?" Issa ventured.

"We were," he said. His tone changed, though, and she could tell that she'd touched on the grief of losing his wife. "We were good for each other. I guess that's what made it easier to stay away from the families. We were happy enough in our own little world."

"While it lasted."

Hutch nodded. "While it lasted," he agreed sadly. "Then about a year and a half ago, Iris had a skiing accident and everything crashed right along with her," he said quietly.

Issa gave him a moment, knowing that if he didn't continue talking about this on his own, she couldn't push him to.

"It was a bad time," he said then, his voice gruff. "And I didn't handle it well."

That sounded like a confession, but she couldn't imagine what he was confessing to. "I think everyone just copes as best they can in a situation like that," she said.

"Nah, I dropped the ball," he disagreed. "I slept for days at a time. I didn't sleep at all for days at a time. I went on booze benders. I didn't eat. I didn't shave. I bit people's heads off. But worst of all, friends had to step in to take care of Ash."

"You weren't up to it," Issa allowed.

"No, but I should have been," he said, clearly not forgiving himself or accepting her excuse for what he'd done. "Instead, for months I wasn't really his dad. I wasn't even thinking about him. I was thinking about myself, feeling sorry for myself. There were times when I wasn't even sure which friend he was with or where he was or if he was being taken care of the way he should have been…" Hutch's expression was filled with self-loathing. "You want to talk about not being a good parent? Believe me when I tell you that your being a little inept or inexperienced can't compare to the kind of parent I was after Iris died."

"Ash doesn't seem any the worse for wear," Issa pointed out, feeling sorry for Hutch in spite of his condemnation of himself.

"Luckily I had good friends who made sure of that."

"And you're a great dad now. Grief made you lapse a little. I think it was understandable," Issa said to comfort him.

He chuckled wryly and squeezed her shoulder with the hand that had been resting atop the sofa back. "Iris would *not* have said that," he declared even though he seemed to appreciate it from Issa. "That was how I finally came out of the clouds. One day I woke up, realized that I didn't have any idea where Ash was or how long it had been since I'd even seen him, and it struck me that Iris would have been so mad at me for that. That the same way she'd made me step up my game with the stores, she would have expected me to step up with Ash no matter what. That I was all he had left and that I couldn't just wallow."

"So you stopped." She just hoped he didn't stop clasping her shoulder because it felt so warm and delicious.

"I stopped wallowing, yeah, and got ahold of myself. It took some time for me to learn everything I needed to know—that *laid-back* part of me had meant that Iris had done pretty much all the caretaking when it came to Ash and I didn't know much about it. But thanks to the same friends who had been looking after him, who took me under their wings to basically teach me how to do what Iris had been doing before, I actually became a hands-on dad." He squeezed her shoulder again. "And that's why I understand where you're coming from— being at sea about what to do with a kid."

"And you're passing on the good deeds done for you by teaching me what your friends taught you?"

"It seems only fair."

"And the family feud? That didn't even end when you lost your wife? When you needed help with Ash?"

"I was wallowing, remember? The last thing I wanted was to deal with anything but my own misery, the personal hell I sort of locked myself up in. So I didn't put out any public notice of Iris's death and I made sure her memorial was small and private. My own family didn't hear about Iris's death until long after the fact, through the grapevine. And because I hadn't gotten ahold of them to tell them, Ian has said that that made them think I didn't want their help. I did let Iris's brother know because that just seemed like the right thing to do."

"What was his reaction?"

"It hit him hard and there were big, big regrets. It took him a while to get on top of his guilt, to stop kicking himself for the time he'd lost with Iris. Then he asked that he be allowed to get to know Ash."

"Did you agree to that?"

"I did. We've gotten together since then, so Ash knows him now. And ultimately I saw his point when it came to my own family—my father is getting older, something unexpected could happen to Ian, and I thought more about ending up with the kind of regrets Dwayne was left with over Iris. About that time I heard from Chase and Shannon, and I learned about my history, that I had other siblings. I was considering mending fences, anyway, so when I got the invitation to Shannon and Dag's wedding, I figured that was an opportunity to get the ball rolling and I probably shouldn't pass it up. We've been working at putting it all behind us ever since."

He said that as if it concluded the story, but Issa was still a little concerned about him, so she said, "And is everything behind you? The grief and all? Do you feel okay now or are you just keeping it to yourself?"

"No, I'm really doing okay," he said, looking pointedly at her as if she had something to do with that.

Then he smiled in a way that told her they were going to put that conversation behind them, too, and said, "It just hit me—where were you for Shannon and Dag's wedding? I know I wouldn't have overlooked you if you'd been there, too."

Apparently he was doing okay enough to flirt.

"While you were enjoying my brother's wedding, I was sitting on my packed bags at the Seattle airport in a storm that had grounded all flights. I couldn't get here."

"Or we would have met then," he said as if the idea intrigued him.

If she had made it to Dag's wedding, they would have met literally days before her disastrous one-night stand with her former boyfriend. Before she'd gotten pregnant.

If only...

"Things might have been different," she heard herself say wistfully.

"Yeah, they might have been. Someone would have introduced us at the wedding, and I would have just been another in a long list of strangers you wanted to shy away from, and I might not have ever gotten to know you."

Ah, another perspective.

"Yes, but would that have been much of a loss?" Issa joked.

"Oh, I think it would have been," he contended. "And I'm just glad that isn't what happened."

His hand trailed from her shoulder to slip under her free-falling hair to the side of her neck where he began a massage that was so soothing, so soft, so sensual that it almost made her purr.

Issa looked into Hutch's sky-blue eyes then, searching for signs that he wasn't over the wife they'd been talking so much about tonight. But she didn't see any. Instead she saw appreciation and desire that verged on raw hunger. For her and her alone.

It went right to her head. Just moments before he leaned forward and kissed her.

She kissed him back, wondering if she should have more compunctions about it. But she just didn't. He'd loved his wife—she didn't doubt that. But she also didn't doubt that he'd waged his war with grief and won. And that somehow having arrived where he was in the aftermath, with her, was what mattered now.

His other arm came around her to bring her to him, closer tonight than last night because as his tongue slid home to hers, her breasts met his chest and made her realize that her nipples had become tiny pearls within the confining knit of her dress. Tiny, oh-so-sensitive pearls...

Apparently it wasn't only her breast size that had increased—so had the way her breasts felt as every nerve ending seemed on the surface, begging for more than the pressure of his pectorals.

With their mouths open wide and seeking, the heat turned up on that kiss. His hand at the back of her head held her to the intensity of it as tongues played a sexy game.

Issa's arms snaked under his and went around him to the wonders of his broad, broad shoulders. She pressed her palms to them, and then pulled his shirt from his waistband to boldly let her hands glide up underneath to the sleekness of his bare back.

Instinct—that's what had prompted her move—the instinct that was crying out for the feel of skin. The feel of his skin beneath her hands, and hers beneath his. And because he didn't seem to mind that bit of intimacy she'd just initiated, she merely enjoyed the delights of smooth silky skin over stonelike muscle and yearned for a little more from him in return....

Only it wasn't her back that wanted his touch so much she could hardly bear it; it was her breasts. Breasts that felt swollen with yearning as those pearled nipples nudged insistently at him, getting more and more aroused by the minute.

His free hand was resting on her waist and it began to rise up her side, building her hopes the higher he got, the closer to the outer swell of her breast. Her breath caught in anticipation until he actually did bring his hand around to the front, encasing her breast in it.

She tried not to let her breath out in a sigh of pleasure, but it wasn't easy because nothing had ever felt quite that good or been quite that perfect a fit.

Her spine arched, insinuating her breast even farther into his grasp, letting him know how good what he was doing felt as their tongues continued to joust and Issa began to shed clothes in her mind.

His clothes and hers, but hers especially because even though his hand was underneath the sequined shrug, her dress and its built-in bra were still between them. And oh, she needed to feel his bare hand against her bare breast.

Maybe she should unbutton his shirt and yank it off. Then if that wasn't enough to let him know what she wanted, what she needed, maybe she should get out of that shrug, tug the front of her dress down—or better yet—reach around and unzip it.

Getting rid of clothes—that was the best idea she'd ever had and everything in her body seconded it.

Until she thought it through a little more.

She'd decided to let what was between them come to a natural conclusion. But maybe the natural conclusion that this was about to take wasn't what she should let happen.

Her body shouted that she was wrong. Every single inch of it wanted that man and wanted him right then and there.

But was that what she should let happen regardless of how much she wanted it to?

Ash was just in the other room. And there were so many complications. So many things that said no even as her body screamed yes!

But she really did hate the thought of his son coming out and finding them.

And the last time she'd been in this position, she'd made a really bad choice. She'd wanted to kick herself afterward. She'd never been so sorry she'd done anything—and that was even before she'd learned the consequences....

She didn't want that to happen again. She didn't want to be sorry for anything to do with Hutch. For anything she ever did with Hutch. And if she had any doubts, if she wasn't sure this was what she should do, she knew she shouldn't do it. No matter how much she might want to.

So she didn't unbutton his shirt and yank it off, she didn't get out of that shrug, she didn't tug the front of her dress down or reach around and unzip it. She just gave herself another scant moment of reveling in the feel of his hand where it engulfed the upper mound of her breast above the dress.

But she knew she couldn't give herself more than that scant moment or her willpower would be lost. Instead, just before that happened, she took her own hands out from under his shirt, bringing them around to press lightly against him as her tongue retreated from the sexy sparring she'd been brazenly engaged in until then.

Message sent and received.

Hutch brought their kiss to an end and let his hand drop to her waist again.

"No?" he asked in a raspy, disappointed voice.

Issa shook her head before it fell to his shoulder. "I keep worrying that Ash might come out," she said to his glorious chest, giving only one of the reasons that had kept her from what her body was still crying out for.

"Yeah, he could do that," Hutch confirmed.

"And I don't want either of us to be sorry," she heard herself confess.

Hutch didn't say anything to that. He merely turned his head to hers and gave her a kiss that lingered. He kept his face in her hair for a long, tender moment that left her uncertain whether his silence meant that he, too, wasn't so sure they should take this any further, or that he understood and was merely honoring her wishes.

Regardless, she closed her eyes the way she had when they'd been kissing and just let the warmth of his breath wrap around her.

But she knew she couldn't indulge in that for long, either, and so with a resigned sigh she sat up straight, away from Hutch.

Issa looked at that handsome face, then, into those blue eyes that let her know that he wanted her as much as she wanted him, and it almost made her rethink the whole thing.

But she forced herself to stand before she lost that battle.

She went to his apartment door with him following behind. He leaned in front of her to open it, then stood gripping the top of it, his long arm and the side of his big body riding its edge. But he caught her hand with his free one before she could step out into the hallway and pulled her to stand close in front of him.

"Are we still on for taking Ash to the Children's Festival tomorrow?" he asked, repeating plans they'd made earlier at the reception.

"Sure," Issa answered, standing in his shadow, breathing in the cool, clear scent of his cologne and dying to wrap her arms around him and bury her face in his chest.

"Ash and I will come get you a little before noon so we can be there for the parade. Does that work for you?"

"It does," she said, struggling to sound normal.

"Good."

That was settled, there was no more to say, and yet he didn't let go of her arm. He just went on looking down at her with an expression that let her know he was fighting plenty himself.

Then he pulled her forward and bent down enough to kiss her again—long and deep, making it all the more difficult for her not to just melt against him.

But he didn't tempt her too far before he ended that oh-so-sexy kiss and took his hand away.

"I don't think it would have been a mistake," he said in a soft, husky voice that was for her ears alone.

"Maybe not. I just didn't know," Issa whispered back.

But before either of them said or did anything else, she went out into the hallway, up the steps and into her own apartment.

Where she locked the door in a hurry just to keep herself from going back downstairs to Hutch.

And to what she wanted more than she might have ever wanted anything before.

Chapter Nine

"**D**id you see that?" Issa gasped. "That redheaded boy just pushed Ash down and took his bucket!"

"Whoa, hold on," Hutch said quietly, keeping Issa seated on the park bench with a hand on her arm.

They'd had a great day at the Children's Festival. The events had kicked off at noon with a parade of kids dressed as their favorite characters walking their pets or riding decorated bicycles, tricycles, scooters or pulling wagons down Main Street to Town Square. In the Square there were more events, games and booths all aimed at children, and Issa and Hutch had taken Ash to all of them, including the display of snakes, spiders and rodents that Issa had hated.

By four o'clock they'd ended where Ash wanted to end it—the communal sandbox. Hutch had told his son that he could have a little while to play with the other kids before they needed to get home. The two-and-a-half-year-old had been doing that under the watchful eyes of his father and Issa. They were sitting on a bench on the sidelines when Issa saw the redheaded boy push Ash down and take the bucket he'd been filling with sand to pour out again.

"That's not right," Issa insisted. "Bullying can't be tolerated."

"I know you're coming from the standpoint of a school system and I'm figuring that you probably always had to step in to stop it there—"

"And Ash is just a baby and that redheaded boy is older and bigger."

"Not much older, and only an inch or so and a couple of pounds bigger. They're a pretty even match," Hutch pointed out. "I appreciate that you care, but let's give Ash a minute and see how he does on his own."

After a moment of being stunned by what the other boy had done, Ash seemed to give it some thought while he took in the fact that the other boy was now filling the bucket with sand and pouring it out to make a competing mountain.

Ash got up, said a very firm, "Not nice! I doan wanna pay with you!" and picked up another, bigger bucket to return to what he was doing, apparently finding victory in the fact that his mountain was already larger.

When the redheaded boy came to take that bucket, too, Ash effectively kept it away from him. "Go 'way! I tol' you, I doan wanna pay with you!"

At that point the redheaded boy's mother stepped in and said, "That's what you get, Lucas. If you can't play nice, no one wants to play with you, and now we have to go home. Tell that boy that you're sorry for taking his bucket and pushing him."

The redheaded boy protested, but his mother insisted, and after a muttered and begrudging "Sowwy," mother and child left the sandbox.

"He handled that pretty well," Issa said when they were gone.

"Yeah, you just never know. That's why I like to give him a chance first. But thanks for playing Mama Bear," he teased, nudging her with his shoulder.

"It was probably dumb," Issa said, slightly embarrassed by her reaction.

"Nah," Hutch answered as he glanced at the huge clock above the door of the city and county building that could be seen from where they were sitting. "We should get going, though. What are you doing in about two hours?"

"Sunday night? Hmm, let's see, I changed my sheets this morning, so I was scheduled for an exciting night of laundry."

"Could you do that during the next couple of hours and then be free?"

Free and hoping he might suggest they do something together.

But Issa kept that to herself and merely said, "I believe so."

"Then how about I show you one more of the joys of parenthood?"

She would take his company in whatever way she could get it and she supposed it was better that it came in the form of their agreement for him to teach her what to do with kids. "Okay."

"It will include some succulent steaks I'll throw on

my barbecue grill and bring upstairs when they're finished, but I never know what to have with them."

Issa took the hint. "So you'd like me to have maybe a side dish, a loaf of bread, things to go with the steaks to make a meal of them?"

He grinned. "A meal... What a terrific idea!" he said as if the suggestion came as a complete surprise. "Is that something you might be interested in?"

Issa laughed. "I think I might be," she said, knowing she'd have to make a quick trip to the general store that served Northbridge's most every need. But she was willing to do it to have dinner with Hutch. And Ash, of course.

"Then we're on," he concluded before he called to Ash to go.

"Min-it," Ash called back.

"No, not in a minute. Now," Hutch said.

Ash pretended not to hear him and ultimately Hutch had to physically retrieve his son from the sandbox before they could take a loudly protesting Ash home.

But Issa didn't pay much attention to Ash's tantrum because she was busy planning how to get shopping, cooking, showering and changing clothes into the next two hours.

It was actually two hours and forty minutes before Issa began to smell steaks cooking on Hutch's barbecue in the backyard, and closer to three hours before she peeked out her kitchen window and saw him take the steaks off.

She was glad for the extra time because her potatoes weren't quite baked yet and it gave her the chance to spruce up her bathroom after her shower and shampoo, and to put away the curling iron she'd used on her hair so she could leave it loose around her shoulders.

Post-shower she'd changed from the T-shirt and jeans she'd had on during the day into a gray-and-white polka dot sundress. It was her favorite—cap sleeves, a U-shaped neckline and four oversize white buttons down the front to close the slightly fitted bodice that eased into a flared skirt.

She'd used a little mascara and lip gloss, but the continued natural rosiness of her cheeks allowed her not to bother with blush. She also didn't bother with shoes because she was staying in her own apartment and it felt good to be barefoot after the day on her feet at the festival.

She was surprised, though, when she opened her apartment door in answer to Hutch's knock and found him there with a plate of steaks and no son.

"Where's Ash?" she asked, peering beyond him into the hallway.

Hutch grinned. "He's having a sleepover with your niece—or I guess Logan's daughter would be your *half* niece."

"So no joy-of-parenting lesson tonight?"

His grin grew. "That's the lesson—the joy of a night off parenting when your kid is away on a sleepover. Everybody needs a breather now and then."

Issa laughed. "You knew all along," she accused.

His only answer was that grin that stayed on his handsome face.

But it wasn't as if Issa wasn't happy to have Hutch all to herself tonight. Or to know that he'd manipulated things so he could have her all to himself. So she swung aside, ushering him in, and closing the door behind him.

He led the way to the kitchen with Issa following behind, enjoying the rear view. He'd changed clothes, too, and likely showered because the scent of soap and his cologne wafted back to her in his wake. Not that his clothes were too much different from what he'd had on earlier—the jeans he was wearing now were merely more faded, and rather than a polo shirt, the T-shirt he had on was bright white and crew-necked with long sleeves that were pushed up above his elbows.

Comfortable—that's how Issa felt and how Hutch looked. Comfortable and so casually sexy.

"I have baked potatoes," she announced as they reached the kitchen section of the apartment. "One for you and one I was going to share with Ash. I also have all the toppings to go with them, a salad and a loaf of Italian bread. But the bakery was closed by the time I got there, so there's no dessert."

"I had enough sweet stuff today—cotton candy, funnel cakes, snow cone, fried marshmallows—dessert doesn't even sound good after all that. But if you want a pudding cup, I have some of those downstairs. I can go get you one."

"Actually I'm kind of sugar-saturated, too, so I think I can pass on the pudding cup. But I've been smelling the steaks for a while now and they're making my mouth water."

Issa took the potatoes from the oven, retrieved the salad from the refrigerator and brought out a pitcher of lemonade, too.

As they tasted everything, exchanged compliments for their separate contributions and then settled into eating, Issa said, "I'm sorry about overreacting at the sandbox today."

"You're sorry that you cared enough about my kid to want to rescue and defend him? I don't think that's anything to apologize for. I appreciated it. And I also think that you should look at it as a good sign."

"That I jumped the gun and wanted to push a little kid down and steal back Ash's bucket?" Issa exaggerated because, of course, she never would have pushed a child or taken something from him.

"Those were instincts, baby, instincts," he said, making her laugh with his over-the-top delivery. "Just when you thought you didn't have any—or maybe you've developed them—either way, that's what that was. A mother's instincts to protect her young. Or in this case, *my* young. I should be thanking you."

Issa hadn't thought of it like that. Instead she'd been afraid she might have embarrassed herself.

"Actually," Hutch went on, "I think you've come a long way in the parenting department. You still need some new-baby techniques and you can probably get those from a class through the hospital. But when it comes to a two-and-a-half-year-old, you were right in there today when it came to wiping Ash's face and sticky hands, and keeping him from running after that cat in the wagon in the parade. I didn't even notice that he was about to do that. You weren't so great keeping him from trying to pet the snake, but—"

"Oooh, *snakes,*" she said with a shudder. "And when you let him hold that big hairy spider…" Another shudder.

"We'll hope you have a girl. Boys like that stuff," he teased. "But otherwise, you're right in there with the best of us watching after a kid. You were at Jenna's farm on Thursday, too, and at the wedding, and today you even caught Ash before he stuck that piece of previously chewed gum in his mouth."

A third shudder. "He picked that up off the ground! I thought he was going to put it in the trash before someone stepped on it and instead he was going to *chew* it!"

"Yep, and he's all mine, that kid," Hutch said facetiously, making her laugh again. "How about from your side—are you more confident? More relaxed? Are you thinking yet that you might be able to do the job?"

Issa thought about it. She wasn't vastly more confident or relaxed or sure yet about motherhood. But she'd made some strides in that direction, so she said, "A little, yes."

"And you've won lots of points with Ash," Hutch said, finishing his steak but leaving some of the rest of his dinner while Issa did the reverse—leaving some steak in favor of finishing half of the potato she'd allotted herself and having a second piece of bread and butter.

"He did do a lot of taking my hand to pull me to the next booth or exhibit," Issa said, secretly pleased by that fact.

"And the only reason the *Itta doll* got to stay home was because you were going to be with us—that was how I persuaded him to leave it behind. But he took it with him tonight. He hasn't been to sleep without it since he got it. You and Za-Za the floppy lion now both share his bed. Lucky little bugger…"

He said that last part under his breath, but it made Issa smile.

"Anyhow," Hutch continued then, "I don't think you

have much to worry about when it comes to being a parent. But here's tonight's lesson—it's tough to get away from your kid, and on the few occasions when you do, it's also tough not to spend that time away talking about your kid. So I'm putting a stop to it here and now. For tonight, no kids, no parenting, no more talking about kids or parenting. We're just you and me."

Just you and me.

That concept was particularly pleasing suddenly. Hutch had basically arranged for this to be a date and while some manipulations and machinations had been involved in accomplishing it, and while they weren't going anywhere, it *was* a night of just the two of them.

"Okay, just you and me," Issa agreed as she stood to clear the table.

Hutch helped and in the course of cleaning up their meal mess, they talked about his grilling skills and Issa's lack of experience in that area.

Then they took their refilled lemonade glasses to the living room where they stood for a while at the window watching the brilliant pink sunset before they turned to the sofa.

They ended up sitting angled toward each other in the center of it, lemonade glasses on the coffee table, Hutch's elbow perched atop the cushions with his attention all focused on Issa.

"Let's do *have you ever*..." he said then with a mischievous twinkle in his sky-blue eyes.

"Have you ever?"

"Uh-huh. I get to ask you a *have you ever,* you have to answer with total honesty, then you get to ask me a *have you ever* and I have to answer with total honesty."

"Like Truth-or-Dare but without the dare."

"No choice but to answer," he challenged.

"I'm a mousy small-town girl."

"You may not be outgoing, but mousy? I don't think so," he corrected.

"Still… How many deep, dark secrets do you think I have?" Issa asked with a laugh.

"Oh, I'll bet there's a few," he answered with a heavy dose of suspicion in his tone.

"Okay," Issa conceded. "But you may beg me to stop five minutes from now."

He merely grinned and said, "Have you ever shop-lifted?"

Issa laughed again. "Okay, you've got me. Yes, once, when I was four. Bright purple star-shaped sunglasses with glitter all around the frames."

"Flashy," he decreed.

"I know. I can't even tell you why something that would make me stick out so much appealed to me. But I wanted them *desperately*. My mother had said no, so when she wasn't looking I pocketed them. Of course, when I put them on on the drive home—"

"Oooh, not wise," Hutch said with a laugh.

"I was *four*," she reminded him.

"And your mother made you return them, confess, apologize and accept whatever punishment the store wanted to inflict?"

"Oh, no. There was no way she was admitting that I'd done something as *low-class* as steal. Word might have gotten around and it would have ruined her better-than-everyone image. She took the sunglasses, ranted and raved at me until I wished I would have just had to go to jail, put them on the floor, smashed them with her foot and threw them away. Apparently it had an effect because I never stole anything again." Issa took a sip of her lemonade. "Now you, have you ever shoplifted?"

"Never," he said as if that gave him one-up on her.

"So *I* had the more interesting story?" Issa said as if his clean record wasn't such an achievement.

"You did," Hutch said, laughing this time. "Okay, have you ever gone skinny-dipping?"

She could feel her cheeks heating just thinking about it. "Once," she admitted in a whisper that made him laugh again.

"And?" he encouraged.

"My friends and I were having a sleepover one summer when I was eleven. It was August, hot, we were sitting beside a pond on the property and someone suggested we just go for a swim. We didn't want to get our clothes wet. The suggestion was made that we just close our eyes, take them off and get in."

"If you say you were the only one who closed her eyes and stripped down and they made you the brunt of a joke, I'm going to hate this," he said ominously.

"No, we all closed our eyes and stripped down. And got into the water. And while we were swimming and giggling and feeling very daring and naughty, a raccoon was sneaking in to take our things. By the time we saw him and chased him away the only thing left was a shoe and a pair of one of the other girls' underwear."

"You got punked by a raccoon?"

"And then we had to walk across the property to the house in the buff and hide in the bushes while our hostess went in for clothes. I never did that again. You?"

"Yes, but again you get more points for color. The worst that happened to me was that the cops came, turned their backs while we—all of us guys—got out and got dressed. Then they just sent us home with a reprimand."

"I suppose that's the difference between country life and living in a gated community," Issa said.

Hutch laughed. "One of many." He paused a moment, then said, "Okay, let's see. Have you ever kissed a stranger?"

"Yes."

Hutch laughed again, a full, barrel-chested laugh. "Really?"

"Thought you were going to stump me with that one, did you?" Issa asked. "Actually, a stranger kissed me. It was a bar bet when I was in college. Some guy I didn't know came up, grabbed me and planted an awful wet one on me. What about you? Have you ever kissed a stranger?"

"Yes, on a dare in high school, after a football game," Hutch answered. "The other team had a cheerleader so incredible-looking we were all drooling. I was trying to play it cool, so one of my teammates called my bluff."

"And you went over and kissed a cheerleader you didn't even know?"

His grin was mischievous again. "I did. My old man saw it and went nuts. He delivered one of the more memorable Morgan Kincaid rants about the vulnerability his position put us all in, and how something like that could be considered assault and I could be arrested, charged, it could make the papers, yada-yada-yada."

"And you didn't care?"

"I just didn't think it was as big a deal as my father did. Especially because the cheerleader had given me her phone number and told me to call her."

"I got slobbered on and you got a date? There's no justice!"

Hutch merely grinned and unbent the elbow that rested on the sofa back so he could run an index finger from her temple to her ear where he swept her hair behind it and began to fiddle with one of the waves.

"Have you ever had an obsession?" he asked then, his voice quieter and more mysterious.

"I don't know," she answered uncertainly because for some reason, that question hadn't sounded as straightforward as the others. "Are we talking eating nothing but graham crackers for a month when I was a kid? Because I've been told I was obsessed with those. And I *have* graham crackers if you want one."

His smile was as mysterious as his tone had been. "No, I'm not talking graham crackers. I'm talking something bigger than that. For instance, I'm beginning to wonder if I'm having an obsession now. I'm not ordinarily an obsessive kind of guy. But lately..." He shook his head as if in disbelief. "I can't seem to shake you."

"Have I been taking up too much of your time?" she asked, unsure if she should be alarmed although it didn't seem like it.

"You have," he said. "Not you, exactly. But I do keep starting things one minute and the next thing I know I'm staring off into space fantasizing about you instead. It's gotten so bad that this morning Ash took my face in his hands like this—" Hutch demonstrated by cupping her cheeks in his palms "—and he held my head so I couldn't look at anything but him when he asked for his cereal for about the sixth time. I'd gotten a bowl down and stopped. Gotten out the cereal box and stopped.

Gotten out a spoon and stopped. By the time I was standing at the refrigerator thinking about kissing you last night, Ash had lost patience. He pulled a chair over and did this."

"That does sound kind of obsessive," Issa whispered, unable to suppress a delighted smile.

With his hands still bracketing her cheeks, she couldn't look at anything but Hutch's handsome face. So that's what she did—studying the faint lines that etched the corners of his sky-blue eyes, that dimple in his chin, those lips that were tantalizing and irresistible and agile and so, so talented.

"Should you see a psychiatrist?" she asked him in jest.

"The cure just seems to be being with you and I like that a whole lot better than the idea of a shrink," he countered, continuing to hold her face while he tipped his own so he could press those supple, agile, so, so talented lips to hers.

And they *were* supple and agile and so, so, sooo talented that the moment she felt their touch, her eyes closed and her own lips responded with an answering kiss.

His hands went into her hair then, continuing to hold her head to that kiss as their lips parted and his tongue found its way to hers.

And as if what had happened between them the night before had only been placed on pause, that single kiss was all it took for everything he inspired in Issa to come into play again.

For the sake of comfort and coolness she hadn't worn a bra and her nipples turned instantly into pebble-hard crests that strained against the soft cotton of her sundress. They were striving for his touch, and to feel that touch without the barriers that had kept her from fully experiencing it the previous evening.

Mouths went wide without any hesitation and tongues reacquainted themselves, impulsive and uninhibited as Issa realized that her hands had found their way to his pectorals once again and she was kneading and massaging them much the way she craved herself.

A little self-conscious about that, she forced her hands to trail up and over his broad shoulders, pressing his back.

His hands came out of her hair then, too. One of them went down to her back, spread out to brace her as that kiss deepened and grew more intense, while the other landed on the side of her waist, inspiring hope.

Up an inch, then two—that was the course of the hand at her side while within the confines of her dress her breasts seemed to expand hopefully.

Only a hint of disappointment came when he finally did reach her breast, enclosing it only on the outside of her dress, leaving fabric between them once again and eliciting a faint sigh from Issa.

She reached for the hem of his T-shirt then, slipping underneath it to the sleek skin of his bare sides.

Was he ticklish? Issa wasn't sure when she felt him smile mid-kiss, when she heard the soft chuckle that echoed from his throat.

Or maybe he merely got the message because then he went from breast to button and made quick work of those four oversize fasteners, leaving the front of her dress agape.

Issa took a deep breath, knowing that her expanding lungs would widen the opening in her dress, and aiming for exactly that.

But before she could burst from her dress, Hutch's big hand slipped inside of it and finally she felt the calloused and slight roughness of his palm close around her, skin to skin.

A tiny gasp escaped her at that first sensation, at her second realization of just how newly sensitive her breasts were. Sensitive enough to drive her almost wild with the wonders he was working there. Wild enough for her to know at that moment of first contact that had it come to this the night before, she would never have been able to call a halt to it.

But she *had* called a halt to things the night before and that gnawed at the edges of her mind.

There had been Ash in the next room—she recalled that that had been a factor. But tonight Ash was off on a sleepover.

And there had been the fear of regretting doing with Hutch what she'd desperately regretted doing the last time she'd done it.

But what was it that Hutch had said just before he'd left Saturday night? That he didn't think it would have been a mistake.

And now, in the moment, she had to agree with that. Because how could anything that felt as good as that strong hand on her breast, as good as those nimble fingers delicately pinching and circling her nipple, be a mistake?

Plus, she realized when she could make herself think about anything but what he was doing to her, what he was causing to erupt within her, this—tonight—wasn't about being lonely or vulnerable or giving in to that the

way that last time had been two months ago. This—
tonight—was about nothing at all but what she wanted.
And what she wanted was Hutch. To be made love to by
Hutch. To know every inch of him as intimately as she
possibly could. To have him know every inch of her.

And if she let that happen, she suddenly knew without question that she wouldn't be sorry for it.

She broke away from their kiss so she could pull his
shirt up and over his head to take it off. And as she did,
she said, "You were right. It wouldn't have been a mistake. It won't be."

That made him laugh—a throaty, masculine rumble
that brought out something even more primitive in Issa
as he paid no attention to her undressing of him and instead sought out her mouth again the moment he could,
leaving her to toss aside his shirt.

But when that kiss began again, there was something
new and different to it. Something untamed, unleashed.
Something more aggressive and commanding, but only
in the most arousing way.

His hand at her breast grew firmer, too. His massage, his kneading and teasing and tormenting lacked
anything tentative at all now.

Then he abandoned her mouth at the same moment
that he freed her breast from her dress and kissed a slow
path down the column of her throat, down the center of
her chest until he reached that swollen orb and drew it
in.

Hot and moist, the inside of his mouth encasing her
breast was like black velvet. And his tongue flicking
against her nipple, tracing it, meeting it tip-to-tip felt
so good that her back arched, begging for more.

Her hands were in his hair—short and dense and

coarse. Then she trailed along wide, wide shoulders that rippled with muscle.

His mouth gave equal time to her other breast and somehow that felt even better as desire ran rampant through her.

But suddenly it all ended and he was gone. He got up, stood beside the sofa and bent over to scoop her up as if she weighed nothing.

"Oh!" was all Issa could say as her arms rounded his neck.

Then he caught her mouth with his to kiss her again while he carried her to the bedroom where he laid her gently on the bed to give her tongue one more tantalizing dance before he was gone again.

Slightly stunned and wondering whether to turn on the light or move to pull back the covers, Issa instead merely watched in rapt, mesmerized interest as Hutch threw off shoes and socks, and peeled down jeans and shorts in the glow of the moon that came through her window.

She was aware of her eyes widening at that first glimpse of him completely naked before her, but she couldn't curb her expression—the man was just too magnificent in all his glory. Honed and toned and perfectly proportioned, and so obviously wanting her.

He wasted no time walking onto the mattress on his knees, straddling her, his hands reaching beneath the cap sleeves of her still-open dress to finesse it from her shoulders and downward until he could cast it away with his jeans, leaving her in nothing but the tiny lace string bikini panties she was wearing. But not for long because he hooked his thumbs into the sides and pulled those off, too.

And like so many other times with this man, Issa somehow felt no shyness, no awkwardness. Instead she didn't mind at all that he spent a moment devouring her with admiring eyes before his hands went flat to the mattress on either side of her head and he lowered himself far enough to kiss her again.

Mouths were wide and urgent now, and as Issa's tongue met and matched Hutch's every thrust and parry, she indulged herself by letting her hands explore him from those athlete's shoulders to the small of his back, to his taut derriere, down the backs of his massive thighs and then around to their fronts and up again.

He didn't even try to hush the groan that she provoked when she first found that long, hard, thick staff. But he did stop kissing her, resting his weight partially on his side in favor of returning to her breast, drawing it far, far into his mouth as his hand first ministered to her other breast and then did a little exploring of its own.

Following the curve of her rib cage that hand eased its way between her back and the bed, pulling her toward him and more to her side before it went to cup her rear end, to slide along the length of her leg and bring that leg over his hip. Once it was there, he reached around it and came up between her legs.

And yes, he could make her gasp, too—because she couldn't stop herself when he first touched her, when he first slipped a finger into her. The man had mad skills that stole her breath and left her writhing in his arms, unsure whether she could wait another moment to have him.

Maybe the tightening of her grip around him told

him so, but then his hand was gone, taking hers from around him, too, and weaving his fingers between hers to bring her arm over her head, to lie her flat to the mattress again to come above her much like before and find his way into her with so much more than mere fingers.

His mouth returned to hers, giving her the sexiest kiss she'd ever had while he eased completely into her, filling her with the silken heat of him, doing nothing but flexing against her a time or two in prelude.

And then he began to move, and so did Issa, matching and meeting him that way, too. Rising and falling, finding yet another thing they did well together. Perfectly, in fact.

Clasping his broad shoulders and holding on tight, Issa lost herself in the pure power and passion of what he was awakening in her, of the heights he was taking her to.

And just when she wasn't sure she could bear more, she burst through to the pinnacle, rushing headlong into an explosive, soul-shaking peak that surpassed anything she'd experienced before, holding her for a moment of the most divine, blissful pleasure she'd ever known, while Hutch, too, found his climax and plunged so completely into her that it genuinely seemed as if they'd become one.

Then they both crossed over that peak and began the decline step by deflating step. Hutch pulsed inside of her and grew still. Heavy breaths grew lighter. Issa could feel her racing heart calm, and every ounce of energy and strength drained away.

For a long moment they just stayed still, communicating only body-to-body.

Then Hutch raised his upper half away from her

and braced himself on his forearms, kissing her again deeply, tenderly, intimately, before he stopped and said, "I don't think there was anything about that that was a mistake. Please don't tell me that you're sorry."

She smiled and looked at him from beneath hooded lids, peering into his eyes, feeling him inside of her and wanting to stay just like that forever.

"I won't because I'm not," she whispered, wondering how it could possibly be that even in utter and complete exhaustion she just wanted to do it again. "In fact, if I had anything left, I'd give you some evidence of just how not sorry I am," she joked, tightening herself around him.

Hutch laughed, sounding relieved and dipping his hips into hers just a little. "I'm a big fan of the power nap and what you can accomplish after one," he enticed. "Or there's always the morning if you need more than a nap. I can be flexible."

"More flexible than you've been? Oooh, show me," she challenged.

He merely laughed again, slipped out of her and rolled onto his back. Then he pulled her to his side where she could use his chest as a pillow and conform her naked body to his.

"First a little rest," he decreed. "Then I'll show you anything you want to see."

And it was with that happy thought and the divine feel of Hutch all around her that Issa fell asleep in his arms.

Chapter Ten

"Where my Itta?" Ash demanded the moment Hutch got him out of the SUV when they arrived home Monday evening.

"Oh, she belongs to you now, huh?" Hutch countered with a twinge of unwillingness to share Issa. Even with his son.

Ash ignored him, climbed back into the vehicle and returned with the doll that the two-and-a-half-year-old had dubbed *Itta*.

"Oh, you meant *that* Issa, not the *real* Issa," Hutch said as he ushered his son into the house so he could give him a bath and get him to bed.

It was no wonder that Hutch had assumed Ash had been referring to the real Issa because the real Issa had been even more on his mind than usual since he'd left her late this morning.

Since he'd *reluctantly* left her late this morning.

After spending the night with her. After making love twice during the night and again this morning. After sharing breakfast in bed with her. After having to pry himself away from her to get to the store much, much later than he'd intended to while Ash spent the day with Tia McKendrick.

And now here he was, after having had dinner with Meg, Logan, Chase, Hadley and the kids, home again and instantly jealous over his son sounding proprietary over Issa.

She'd plans to have dinner with an old friend tonight. He couldn't even remember the woman's name. All he knew was that when she'd told him that, when he'd realized that he wasn't going to get to see her tonight, he'd felt deprived. And now he was home and the first thing he'd noticed when he'd driven up was that none of the windows in her place upstairs had light coming from them—meaning that she wasn't there yet.

"Can Itta come ober?" Ash asked as Hutch undressed him once they were inside.

"Nope, it's late and you need a quick bath and to get to bed. You've had a big day."

"I yice Itta," Ash informed him, setting the doll on the counter beside the bathroom sink while Hutch filled the tub. "I yice her lot."

"I like her a lot, too," Hutch agreed with his son when he lifted him into the bath.

"She's pit-tee."

"Yes, she is pretty. Beautiful, in fact."

"Boot-a-ful," Ash repeated, more interested in trying to sink his duck-shaped sponge than in Hutch lathering him up.

But Issa was so much more than her looks, Hutch

thought as he did. There wasn't anything about her that he *didn't* think was great. That he *didn't* enjoy and miss when he wasn't with her.

"Can we see her tomollow?" Ash asked.

"Tomorrow—maybe."

But tomorrow seemed so far away when Hutch was itching to have her there with them right then. And again tomorrow. And the day after that and the day after that and the day after that.

He wanted her around all the time. He didn't want to be away from her at all. Ever.

It was a thought that had been slipping in and out of his mind all day. A thought he'd been skirting because it seemed so unrealistic. But now, with Ash bringing Issa up, too, wanting her there with them, he finally allowed the thought fully into his head.

He wanted her in his life. And not just on a temporary basis. Not just to hang out with or date or anything superficial. He wanted her in his life for good.

Oooh, that made him feel a little guilty. And disloyal to Iris, he realized.

But Iris was gone and nothing could bring her back, he reminded himself. And the rational part of him knew that she wouldn't begrudge him the kind of happiness he felt with Issa. That just wasn't the person she'd been.

But he also knew that Iris would care deeply who raised her son, and having Issa in his life would mean that Ash would have her in his life, too.

How would Iris feel about that?

"Goggles," he told his son, waiting while Ash slipped on his bright red swim goggles so he could shampoo the toddler's hair and rinse it without getting soap or water in his eyes.

Hutch couldn't believe that there was anything about Issa that Iris would have disliked—Issa was a good, kind, decent, caring person, and Iris would have recognized that, appreciated it. It would be exactly what Iris would want in a stepparent for Ash.

Of course, Issa *had* had a bad example of stepparenting in the way her own mother had treated Logan and Hadley, and he couldn't discount that. But Ian had pointed out that Issa was *not* her mother, and Hutch hadn't seen anything in Issa herself that seemed to be the way she'd described her mother, either. So why should he believe she would be that same kind of stepmother to Ash?

And when it came to Ash and what he *had* seen of Issa's treatment of him?

She'd warmed to him almost as fast as he'd warmed to her.

Hutch had watched her yesterday at the Children's Festival, he'd seen how easily she'd accepted it each time his son had taken her hand to drag her to the next booth or exhibit. He'd seen how she'd looked out for Ash and Ash's safety, how she'd kept him out of harm's way, how she'd helped him climb onto the box he'd needed to use to access the ring toss game—it had all been a show of affection, of kindness, of patience.

There had been the show of concern, too—Hutch had had to hold her back to keep her from jumping to Ash's defense when the kid in the sandbox had bullied him. And even before yesterday, when Hutch had had her babysit while he'd gone to the bachelor party, Issa had consoled Ash after his nightmare and then continued to hold him at the expense of her own comfort rather than risk disturbing him. Iris would have been grateful for that.

Okay, mothering might not come naturally to Issa, but she was getting better at it. And she was motivated and she had a genuine desire—not to mention a need of her own—to cultivate whatever nurturing instincts she'd begun to tap into with Ash.

So when he thought about the kind of stepparent Issa would be to his son and whether Iris would approve, he decided that she would. And that rather than taking anything away from Ash by spreading himself thinner—the way Hutch had worried might happen if he got involved with anyone—Issa added to the attention Ash received, the care. With Issa he would again have two parents and that was a good thing.

On the other hand, the reason Issa had a need of her own to cultivate those mothering abilities was because she was pregnant—that wasn't something he could overlook.

Pregnant.

With some other guy's baby.

It was weird, he thought, but even when he wasn't losing sight of the fact that she was pregnant, he never really thought of her baby as someone else's. He only thought of it as hers and hers alone. Which it actually was now that the father had opted so completely out of the picture.

And the truth was, Hutch just didn't think about anyone from Issa's past. Maybe in the same way Iris didn't come to mind whenever he was with Issa— unlike when he'd been with other women since Iris's death—whoever had preceded him didn't seem to loom in the background, either.

Iris was gone, she was part of his history, and the father of Issa's baby was just a part of Issa's history. But when he and Issa were together it was as if something new and fresh and strong was forged between them. Something that really made the past the past, that made what they were creating in the here and now what was most important.

But that still didn't change the fact that if he was considering a future with Issa, he would be taking on her baby the same way she would be taking on Ash—that was no small thing and he thought seriously about it. Weighed it. Imagined it. Pictured himself in that role.

But even when he did, nothing about it disturbed him.

Actually, he kind of liked the idea of going through it all with her, of being there for her, of sharing that experience, and then that child, exactly the way he wanted to share everything with her. Everything in her life. Everything in his.

Plus Ash would have a little brother or sister, and after watching Ash thrive on playing with Tia McKendrick and even with his younger cousin Cody, Hutch thought that Ash might be thrilled to have another kid in the house.

"Under the big waterfall and then we're done," he warned his son as he filled a glass with fresh water and poured it over Ash's head to rinse his hair.

"So you like Issa," Hutch said to Ash when they were finished and he lifted the little boy out of the bathtub.

"I yice her," Ash confirmed.

"Would you like her to be with us all the time? Live with us and be a part of our family?"

"'Kay," the two-and-a-half-year-old agreed. "Now?"

"Well, no, not right now. She still isn't home. But maybe soon."

"'Kay." Then, apparently to show his enthusiasm, in the midst of Hutch drying him off, Ash reached for his doll and planted a big, elaborate kiss on the doll's face.

"Okay…" Hutch said with a laugh at his son's antics, feeling very much like planting a big kiss on the real Issa himself.

And yes, also wanting to have her with them all the time and live with them and be a part of their family, too.

Because what it all boiled down to was that what he felt for Issa was what he'd thought he'd never feel again, what he'd found in her was another person who meant the world to him.

And he couldn't just let that slip through his fingers no matter what.

He couldn't let *her* slip through his fingers.

And he wouldn't.

"Uh-oh, did Ash kick you out?" Issa joked when she went in the main door on Monday night and found Hutch sitting on the stairs that led to her place, his own apartment door open.

"Nope, he dispatched me to go get you, though," the big man joked back.

He slid from the center of the step to one side where he pivoted slightly to put his back to the railing. Then he patted the other half of the step, gesturing for her to join him. "But now he's sound asleep and it's just me who wants you. Come and sit with me, I have something to talk to you about."

"That sounds heavy," Issa said, more than happy to join him.

She just couldn't seem to get enough of the man. They'd spent the night and most of the morning together, and yet the minute he'd left she'd missed him. She'd gone on missing him all afternoon. She'd considered canceling her dinner with her old friend and Neily's sister Mara Pratt just in hope of spending the evening with Hutch instead, but she'd forced herself not to do that. Then, all the way home, she'd wondered—hoped—she might still get to see him tonight, and finding him there on the stairs had sent a thrill right through her.

Of course, the man was always something to behold and that was true even in jeans and a simple gray short-sleeved T-shirt. But there was more to her attraction to him than mere good looks and she gladly sat on the step beside him, turning her back to the wall so she could see him.

"Is something wrong?" she asked.

"Actually, I wanted to talk to you about just how not wrong everything is."

Then he surprised her with more than his presence on the stairs.

She listened as he told her that he had feelings for her that he'd never thought he would have again. Feelings that made him want a future with her. Feelings that made him want to be a part of her future. That made him want to be by her side through having her baby, raising it, just the way he wanted her by his side through raising Ash.

"Wow..." she whispered when he slowed the rush of words, when he laughed at himself and went on to tell her all he'd thought about that had brought him to this point.

But by then Issa didn't hear much more because she was lost in her own thoughts.

Hutch was such an amazing man—that was uppermost in her mind as she looked at his chiseled features, at his incredible blue eyes, as she thought about the time they'd spent together since they'd met, about last night.

And she couldn't deny that she had feelings for him, too. Feelings she'd been leery of exploring or looking at too closely, feelings that she thought just might match the feelings he was talking about.

And here he was, offering so much that appealed to her. Himself. His life. Ash. A future together. A future that meant she wouldn't be alone in all she was facing herself.

But that was what triggered caution in her. What set off alarms.

It was one thing that in former relationships she'd compensated for the shortcomings her shyness had left her with with men who could be gregarious and outgoing, who kept anyone from noticing that she stood back, that she was too nervous to be witty or clever, that she was the meek mouse in the corner.

But now it was parenthood on the horizon. And Hutch could easily round out what she might lack in that department.

So what if that was behind her temptation to agree to what he was proposing? she asked herself now. What if that was really the deciding factor? Just how much influence was being brought to bear by her own fears?

By her concerns that she couldn't do this alone? Or that she might do it badly on her own?

As thrown for a loop as she was by this pregnancy, by the thought of having a baby and raising it without any help, that *was* the decision she'd made—*not* to rely on anyone else to help carry the load. To stand on her own two feet no matter how difficult it might be.

But it was daunting. And what if now that Hutch was giving her a way *not* to have to do it all alone, to share the burden, *that* was as much of an enticement as the man himself?

If there was any chance that that was the case, she knew she couldn't say yes. Certainly not to the man who wasn't even the father of her baby. It would just be so unfair.

And at that moment she couldn't be absolutely sure one way or the other....

"I don't think I can let you do that," she said suddenly to keep him from saying any more of the things that were all music to her ears—the things he liked and appreciated about her, that he wanted her so much it had become a driving force in him, all the things that made her willpower, her stamina, her resistance to him weaker by the minute.

"You can't let me do what?" he asked.

"Step up and be a father to a child who isn't yours."

"Why not, if I'm willing? I'm asking you to step up and be a mother to a child who isn't yours—to Ash. My kid will be your kid, too. Maybe later we'll have one or two who are ours."

From there Hutch continued to paint a portrait of a future for them. Of a family. And that just made Issa all the more nervous. Ash and her own baby and then maybe a *third and a fourth?* She didn't even know how well she would mother one child, let alone three or four.

But she did know that the thought of mothering one was intimidating enough. Hutch was better at this than she was. He took it all more in stride—the way he did everything. But that wasn't her nature. Yes, she was going to do her best, she was going to do everything she possibly could to be a good mother to her baby. But to take on Ash, too? And then potentially more?

What if she couldn't handle all of that? Ash could suffer for it. Her own baby could suffer for it.

And what if Hutch had to pick up the ball she dropped, not only with his own son, but with her child, a child who had come from another man? She would feel horrible and like such a failure. And wouldn't he be likely to resent that she couldn't carry her weight? That because of that, time and energy were taken from his own son?

As much as she'd worried at first that she might be inclined to repeat her pattern of having a man in her life round out her rough spots, now she was even more worried about what could come of agreeing to what Hutch was asking of her. Of overextending her limited skills. Of disappointing Hutch and Ash and of letting down her own child even more drastically than she'd feared before.

The whole thing just seemed like a disaster in the making.

"No!" she said, calling a halt to the future he was laying out for them, to all that was running through her mind, to what already seemed like too much for her. "I have to take care of *my* kid, *my*self. That's what I signed on for with this baby, and I'm not even sure I can do that. I can't sign on for Ash, too, and then who knows how many others. I...I can't!"

"It wouldn't be only you, Issa," he reasoned. "We'd be in it together, equal partners, sharing the load."

"But the bigger the load gets, the more I'd be taking on, and the greater the chance that I won't be able to take an equal part. And then you'll have to make up for what I lack and—"

"Okay, okay, don't get upset," Hutch said in a tone that was obviously meant to calm her down because she *was* sounding panicky again—probably because she was feeling panicky again.

He took her hand, wove his fingers between hers and pulled it to rest on his knee. "Think about how good we've been together," he urged quietly. "You haven't stood back when it's come to Ash, you've *stepped up* whenever and wherever it's been called for."

"That was the point—I was learning how to take care of a kid."

"Still, you did it and you got better and better at it. And it's been really nice for me to have someone else there, to keep an eye on him, to help out."

"But then there will be my baby, and maybe another, and—"

"Sure, when the new baby comes we'll have more on our hands and we'll have to make adjustments."

"Adjustments that could take you away from Ash. You told me part of why you moved to Northbridge was to keep distractions from him to a minimum. Now you're talking about much bigger distractions than city living."

"But even if he has a little less from me, he'll have what he gets from you to make up for it, and that's important, too. It all balances out!" Hutch insisted. "We balance each other out."

Issa wished she saw it that way, but she was too afraid that what would be asked of her, expected of her, might be more than she could manage. All she knew for sure at that moment was that she'd already taken on a huge endeavor that she wasn't sure she could do; she couldn't possibly take on more on top of it.

She took a breath and did the first thing she didn't want to do—she pulled her hand out of Hutch's. Then she pushed herself to her feet again.

"I just don't think it's a good idea," she decreed in a voice broken by all the remorse that was mounting inside of her.

Hutch stood, too, taking her by the shoulders, looking deeply into her eyes the way he so often did just before he kissed her.

And having him kiss her was what she wanted him to do in spite of everything, in spite of knowing she really couldn't let that happen now.

And she couldn't. She wouldn't. And knowing that just made her eyes flood with tears she had to fight to keep from falling.

"It isn't all about being parents, you know," Hutch said in a low, gravelly voice. "It's about you and me, too. First and foremost. You're everything to me, Issa. Everything."

And if it was about only the two of them, this could very well be turning out differently, Issa thought. But it wasn't and it never could be. Ash wasn't going to disappear into thin air, and she'd made the decision to have her own baby and she wasn't going to change that now.

So Issa merely shook her head, her eyes stinging as

if they were on fire. "But it isn't *just* about you and me, that's the problem," she whispered before she shrugged out of his grip on her shoulders. "So this can't happen," she concluded, losing the battle with her tears and turning quickly away from him to rush up the stairs, ignoring Hutch calling her name from behind.

But she never turned back.

Instead she let herself into her apartment where she closed and locked her door firmly behind her before the tears came in a flood.

Then all she could do was sink to the floor and try to keep from sobbing while she refused to answer Hutch's knocks on her door or his requests for her to let him in so they could talk more.

Chapter Eleven

"Now tell me what's going on."

It was nearly evening on Tuesday when Hadley sent Chase and Cody home, closed the door to the apartment above the garage on the Mackey and McKendrick compound and turned to Issa to make that demand.

First thing Tuesday morning Issa had called Logan to say that if the offer of staying in the compound apartment until she found a house was still good, she'd like to take him up on it. She hadn't given a reason and while her half brother's silence had waited for one, he hadn't asked her outright why she wanted to make the move from Hutch's duplex. He'd merely said that of course she could stay there, that he and Hadley had wanted that in the first place.

But Logan, Meg and Tia were going to Billings for the day, so Issa's second phone call had been to Hadley to ask if Hadley would help her with the actual move, which luckily—because both apartments were furnished—only involved clothes and small items.

Again Issa had offered no explanation. But with the move accomplished—and with the mention that Issa wanted to get it finished before Hutch got home from work—her half sister was not going to let her off the hook.

"Your eyes are all red and bloodshot, so I know you've been crying," Hadley continued. "You look like you haven't slept. You wouldn't stay here with Logan and me from the start—which was weird. You've been kind of secretive since you got back to Northbridge. And now this. What is going on with you?"

Issa slumped down onto the apartment's easy chair, resting her head on the back cushion as she gave in to confessing, beginning with the fact that she was pregnant, by whom and what had happened with David to leave her on her own with the situation.

"And you didn't think you could tell us?" Hadley said as she sat on the coffee table in front of Issa.

"It's just so humiliating, Had. I shouldn't have given in to the night with David in the first place. It was dumb and—"

"And you're human like the rest of us and we all do dumb things now and then."

"And I *did* make sure there was protection. It just failed, and—"

"It's water under the bridge. The important part is that now there will be a baby and we all like babies!" Hadley said with excitement.

Issa laughed forlornly, appreciating that that was the way her sister was taking this. "But I don't know the first thing about them, or about being a parent, and

Hutch offered to show me the ropes and let me do some practicing on Ash in exchange for house hunting with him and giving him the inside track on Northbridge."

"Ah, that's why the two of you were spending so much time together."

"Well, that and that we… That something started between us…" Issa went on to pour out her heart to her sister about all that had happened with Hutch. And how it had ended and that that was why she'd wanted to make the impromptu move today—because it had just been too painful to stay living so close to him.

"So let me make sure I understand this," Hadley said when Issa had finished and couldn't keep from crying again. "You turned Hutch down because you're worried that you might be depending on yet another man to make up for what you think is a shortcoming in yourself."

"And I'm worried that because Hutch is offering, it's just too easy *not* to do this on my own. I'm worried that I might have wanted to accept just so I don't have to."

"You won't be doing it on your own," Hadley reasoned. "We'll all be right there with you, Issa. I don't care—and I know no one else will, either—how this happened. What matters is that we'll have a new baby in the family and you know that we'll all do whatever it takes to help out."

Issa did know that, but hearing her sister say it only made more tears fall and she went for the tissue box in the bathroom, bringing it back with her.

When she sat down again, Hadley continued, "And besides being afraid that you might be taking the easy way out by saying yes to Hutch, you're also worried that if you do, you still won't be able to handle being a mom to your own baby and a stepmom to Ash and—"

"And more, Hutch was talking about *more* kids, too," Issa said miserably.

Hadley laughed and Issa didn't appreciate that. "What's so funny?"

"He really did blow it talking about even more kids," Hadley observed. "So let's back up. What if there were *no* kids? How do you feel about Hutch?"

"Oh, he's great…" Issa nearly wailed, making her sister laugh again. "I've never felt about anyone the way I feel about him. Ever. He's funny and he's sweet and he's kind and he's generous and he's… He's sooo hot! And when I'm with him I don't want him to leave, and the minute he does, I can't wait to see him again, and I think about him all the time and—"

"Got it," Hadley said to stop the accolades.

But Issa had to add one more. "And I'm better than me when I'm with him."

"What does that mean?"

"I'm calmer, I'm more relaxed and braver."

"He brings out the best in you," Hadley suggested.

"And not only when we're alone."

"I know that I haven't noticed you hiding behind him when I've been with the two of you," Hadley said after she seemed to think about it.

"That's because it's like… It's like I'm more comfortable being myself just because he's there with me. It sounds crazy, but that's how I feel. And that's never happened before. Before it's been that the guy I was with was so *on* that no one noticed what a dud I can be. They were like my cloaking device. But with Hutch, it isn't as if he makes *me* the life of the party, but I feel so much better just being with him that I think I'm actually a little less of a dud, if that makes any sense. But doesn't that make him an even bigger crutch than guys in the past?"

"Someone who brings out the best in you isn't the same as someone who can tell jokes at a party so you can sit in the corner and not be noticed. Bringing out the best in you is a good thing, Issa."

Issa thought about that and it didn't take long for her to see her sister's point and concede to it. "It does feel good," she admitted. But then there wasn't a way in which Hutch didn't make her feel good.

"I also think that maybe he's helping to bring out the best of you when it comes to parenting, too. That that doesn't mean that you were tempted to say yes to him to take the easy way out of it."

"But there *is* still all the parenting stuff," Issa lamented. "The *step*parenting stuff—what if I end up the kind of stepmother my mother was to you and Logan?"

"I know better than anyone what our house was like growing up," Hadley said. "But do you see yourself being like your mother? Do you really think that if you were in a house with Hutch and Ash and your own baby that you wouldn't pitch in, that you'd let yourself slight Ash or your own baby or any other kids?"

The way her mother had slighted Hadley and Logan.

"Not on purpose!" Issa said without hesitation. "But what if I'm a complete idiot when it comes to the whole mothering thing? What if I'm so inept and clumsy and—"

"You won't be because you don't want to be. You told me that Hutch said you're getting better and better at taking care of Ash, at looking out for him, at making sure he gets everything he needs and more. I think you've seen what not-so-great stepparenting is and I know you *don't* want to be that, so you won't be. And you'll be fine with your own baby, too. And even with any others if you decide you *want* there to be others."

"And you don't think I should be worried that having someone else to share the load is the appeal?"

"You think *that's* the appeal of the guy you feel more for than any guy you've ever known? That that's the appeal of the guy who's funny and sweet and kind and generous and sooo hot? The guy you want to be with every minute and can't stop thinking about? Who brings out the best in you?"

The idea of becoming a parent with Hutch holding her hand through it was undeniably a comfort to her. The same way he was a shot in the arm to help tame her shyness, he boosted her confidence on the kid front, too. But to say that his appeal was in that?

Hadley was right. Hutch's appeal was all about Hutch himself, and when Issa honestly thought about it, she knew it.

She also knew that her feelings for him weren't about his parenting skills, that while she'd grown to like Ash and being with him, she'd also been eager to have Hutch to herself, eager for those times when it had been only the two of them. Because it wasn't all about being parents, he'd tried to tell her that last night.

"But what about him taking on a baby that isn't his?" Issa said then, thinking out loud.

"Did you think he was lying when he said he was okay with that?" Hadley asked. "Do you not want to take on Ash?"

The tears finally stopped and as Issa mopped up her face, she considered those two questions.

She believed that Hutch was willing to treat her baby as his own. To be a father to it. He'd already shown more interest, more support than the biological father had. More enthusiasm. And Hutch's tranquil nature, his acceptance of things, the kind of openness he'd shown allowed her to believe that he, of all men, could be a dad to another man's child.

And when it came to Ash? Somewhere along the way the two-and-a-half-year-old had gotten to her enough that she hated the thought of not having him in her life almost as much as she hated the thought of not having Hutch.

"No, I know Hutch wasn't lying and I'm crazy about Ash," Issa said in belated answer to her sister's questions.

And in truth, having hated the way her own mother had treated Hadley and Logan, Issa was determined and motivated to make sure she embraced Ash, that she loved him and showed him that she loved him every bit as much as her own child.

"So I've just been silly?" she asked her sister.

Hadley shrugged. "Unless David is playing a part in anything—do you still care for him? Is there some tiny part of you that hopes he'll change his mind and—"

"No," Issa answered without having to think about it. "David had sucked the life out of my feelings for him before we broke up. That's why I broke up with him. I'd just had enough all the way around. That night two months ago really, really was just a stupid moment of weakness. I wouldn't even want him to change his mind about the baby because then I'd have to deal with him making promises he wouldn't keep and letting the kid down and everything else that would come with the whole David package."

"Then, no, I don't think you've been silly, just maybe a little freaked out, and that's not hard to understand," Hadley assured. "Believe me, I know that when it happens this fast it can knock you off balance."

Balance.

That was what Hutch had said the night before—that they balanced each other out. That it had helped him with Ash to have her around, to have her share the load.

So maybe they could be partners. Equal partners. In everything.

And that was what she wanted, Issa admitted to herself. She wanted Hutch and to share all there was to share with him, good and bad, easy and difficult, with kids or without kids. As long as she had him, nothing was insurmountable.

"Maybe I won't be staying here, after all," she told Hadley. "But I would like to shower and change clothes and make sure I don't look like someone who was up all night and has been crying most of the last twenty-four hours."

"Go for it!"

"Itta! Whe' you bin?"

The main door to Hutch's rental had been unlocked so Issa had let herself in. After standing outside of his apartment door for at least five minutes trying to gain some courage, she'd knocked. It was half an hour past Ash's bedtime, so she'd assumed the toddler would be asleep. But he'd answered the door.

Where had she been?—that was his question and she didn't know how to answer it.

"Oh, I was with my sister," she said vaguely.

"I cu-uered you a pisher. I go ge' it!"

Ash ran off, leaving Issa standing in the hallway, unsure what to do when she heard Hutch's voice call, "Ash? Where are you? You were supposed to go to the bathroom and get right back in bed."

And then there Hutch was, suddenly, at the end of the hallway that led to the bedrooms, straight across the living room from the door.

He stopped short the minute he saw her, staring at her as if he was stunned to see her.

After giving in to Hadley's suggestion that she sit for half an hour with cucumber slices on her eyes to combat the redness that so much crying had left, Issa had showered, washed her hair and left it to fall in loose waves around her face. She'd dressed in her best-fitting jeans and two curve-hugging shirts—a navy blue Henley that she'd left unbuttoned over a lacy white camisole. She knew that nothing about her appearance should have incited any kind of shock. Yet there Hutch was, studying her without saying so much as hello.

Still at a loss for words herself, she muttered, "I knocked and Ash opened the door."

Hutch's only response was to raise his dimpled chin in acknowledgment.

He had on jeans and a pale blue sport shirt that was so crisp that it looked as if he'd just put it on. He was also freshly shaved and the faint scent of his cologne wafted to her and caused her to wonder if he'd been about to go out.

On a date? Could the obstetric nurse have gotten to him in just one day?

That was what flashed through her mind, and despite the fact that it seemed unlikely, it still sent a wave of jealousy through her. Along with a horrible fear that she'd done more damage than she'd originally thought.

Then the front door opened and in came a teenaged girl to support the idea that he was on his way out.

Issa had glanced over her shoulder at the sound of the main door opening and hadn't seen Hutch join her at the apartment door.

But that was where he was when he said, "Hi, Tina. Looks like I won't be needing you, after all, but let me pay you for your trouble."

"I don't want to keep you if you have plans," Issa said quietly.

"My plans were to find you," Hutch finally said to her as he took his wallet out of his back pocket and handed some bills to the girl, who was insisting that he didn't need to do that.

Hutch wouldn't take no for an answer, and after thanking him, the teenager left.

About that same time Ash came charging back to the door with a page torn from a coloring book.

"Yookit, it's you!"

Issa took the sheet of paper he was offering her. On it was the line drawing of a princess haphazardly colored in.

"And you did such a good job coloring," Issa praised.

"Yoo kin hab it."

"I can have it? Thank you," Issa said.

"And you," Hutch told his son firmly, "get back in

your bed and I don't want to hear another peep out of you."

"Nuzzer story?" Ash asked hopefully.

"Nooo! You've been messing around for the last hour and that's it! Go to bed!"

Hutch was usually so patient with the toddler, but now he sounded at wit's end and Issa was afraid she had something to do with that. But Ash didn't seem bothered by it; he just tried another tactic.

"Kin Itta tut me in?"

"You've been tucked in three times. Just go to bed!" Hutch said in more of the stop-fooling-around tone. "Now!"

"'Kay," Ash said petulantly, but he turned and trudged off to his bedroom.

Then it was only Issa and Hutch again.

Hutch curved a long arm behind her to usher her inside the apartment so he could close the door.

Before he said anything he held up a single index finger in a gesture that said *wait a minute*. Then he went back and checked to make sure Ash had done what he was told.

Apparently satisfied with what he found, when Hutch returned he kept some distance from Issa that caused her to worry that he'd reconsidered what he'd been willing to do the night before and changed his mind. That he'd planned to find her tonight to tell her that.

So she said, "You know that I left the keys on the counter upstairs, if that was why you were coming to find me."

After clearing her things out of the upstairs apartment and leaving the keys, she'd slid a note under his door downstairs telling him that she was giving up the place.

"I don't care about keys," he said. "I care about you, although you didn't give me a chance to say what I wanted to say about that last night."

"I know. I sort of flipped out. I'm sorry," she apologized.

Then she took a deep breath and decided that she had to take things from there. So she went on to tell him that she'd thought more about what he'd said, that she'd talked to Hadley who had helped her see everything more clearly and in a better light. That she'd realized she was wrong.

"It does make me feel so much better to think about having this baby with you," she told him. "But only because you make me feel so much better about everything, not because I was falling into an old pattern of needing a crutch. It's just that there's so much that goes along with you and being together and it's all so complicated. I had to mentally take Ash out of the picture, mentally take the pregnancy and the baby out of the picture, and the thought of any future kids, too."

"Yeah, I realized late last night that I'd gotten ahead of myself with that and that it had put you over the edge."

"But when I asked myself what if it was just you and me, what if we'd met when we were both completely free, gotten to know each other, dated, ended up where we were last night, would my reaction have been different?"

"Would it have been?"

"I love you, Hutch," she said in answer to that, not caring that she was saying it first. "When I stripped away everything else, all the complications, when I looked at just you and me, I knew that the bottom line was that I wanted to be with you. To have a future with you. I knew that everything else is just details—and I don't mean that I'm taking it lightly that I'll be Ash's stepmom, I promise you I'll be the best one of those I can possibly be—"

"I know you will be," he assured, crossing to her again and circling her hips with his arms, his hands clasped at the small of her back.

Issa's hands went to his biceps, still keeping some distance between them because she wanted this whole thing sorted through before she got carried away with anything else.

"And I'm not taking for granted, not even for a minute," she continued, "what a big deal it is that I'm going to have a baby that isn't—"

"It's mine if I say I want it to be. And I do."

"Still, I'm not taking that lightly, either. And I promise you that I won't sit on the sidelines when it comes to parenting just because you're already good at it."

He laughed. "Oh, believe me, we'll both need to be in the thick of it for that."

"I just… I lost sight of what there is between us when it's just you and me. I…I panicked," she said, knowing it might be repetitious but at a loss for a better word. "And you may not believe me because I seem to be doing a lot of panicking lately, but I'm not ordinarily that way."

"What I believe is that you're quiet and logical and cautious to go along with all the other things that I love about you. So it's no surprise that you felt overwhelmed—that you *feel* overwhelmed—by what you have on your plate and the idea of adding more. But you saved me the trouble tonight of searching you out so I could tell you that for the first time in my life I've found something I can't take in stride myself—your turning me down. And all I knew was that I had to find you so I could convince you how good we are together and that none of what you were worried about last night matters. That together we can take on anything we need to."

Issa gave in to what she wanted to do herself and moved her hands from his arms to his chest, relaxing enough to ease closer as she smiled up into that face she wanted to wake up to every day for the rest of her life. "*Are* we good together?" she asked because she knew he was good for her and only hoped that she was good for him.

"You're like my own private island getaway. When I'm with you, no problem is as big as it seemed before or matters as much as it did. Food tastes better, the air smells cleaner, colors are brighter and I feel more alive and involved and glad for that than I've felt in a really long time. Even when it comes to Ash, I told you, it's been so nice to have someone by my side with him. And not only to share the work. Somehow having you to share *him* has made me enjoy him more. It isn't as if I can't do the parenthood thing on my own—I have been and I can—but it's easier and more fun and it takes some of the burden and the stress away when there are two of us."

"Hmm...I was worried that I might have been inclined to say yes to you because then I'd have you to carry some of the load for me. But maybe that's why you want me—because *you* need someone to help carry your load," she joked.

"That's it, you've found me out," he said with a grin. "I just need some free child care, cooking, cleaning, laundering, errand running—"

"The truth comes out!" Issa continued the joke.

But then Hutch sobered slightly, looked deeply into her eyes and said, "If you'd given me the chance last night I would have told you that I love you. I love you more than the sun and moon wrapped up together. I love you more than I thought I'd ever be able to love anyone again. I would have told you that I want you to be my wife. And if it takes my getting down on one knee right now to ask you, I'll do it, don't think I won't."

"I haven't read the bylaws, but I believe I can say yes from this angle and it will still be valid," she answered with a smile, feeling her eyes well up again, this time with happy tears that she blinked back because crying was the last thing she wanted to do at that moment.

Hutch pulled her nearer and kissed her then, and Issa knew in that moment that she couldn't have gone on living her life without that kiss. Without having his touch as his hands unclasped from behind her so one could spread out against her back and the other could come to the side of her face to hold her as the kiss went from sweet and poignant to something much more.

There were so many things that she couldn't have lived without, Issa realized then, when desire sprang to life in her almost instantly, when her nipples hardened as that kiss grew urgent and that hand at her cheek began a slow descent to her waiting breast.

Issa knew where this was going. Where every inch of her was already crying out for it to go. But as with that other time when she hadn't let it get there, Ash came to mind.

She ended their kiss to whisper, "Ash is in the next room."

Hutch smiled a devilish smile and kissed her again, briefly, before he said, "Ash is asleep by now or he would have been out here again."

"But he could wake up and catch us."

"Then there would be one of those stories to tell. He's gonna be in the next room—and so is the new baby—for a long, long time. And I'm not doing without you until the kids start college," he said.

But rather than go on with what had begun, he took her hand and led her into his bedroom where he closed the door securely behind them. "Tomorrow we can buy a lock. But until then—" his grin went wicked again "—we live dangerously."

Issa couldn't help laughing at him just before he recaptured her mouth with his and maneuvered her onto his bed where clothes were shed to free the way for kisses, exploring hands and entwined arms and legs.

No, she could never have lived without his touch, she thought as those big, adept hands of his worked their wonders over every inch of her. Or without the chance to work a few of her own wonders over the magnificence that was his smooth skin over toned and taut muscle.

She could never have lived without the feel of her naked body pressed to his, the feel of him slipping inside of her, the feel of the passion he ignited from that moment on.

Powerful, powerful passion that swept through her like wildfire and turned any lingering doubt to dust as she rode with him to the kind of heights she also couldn't have denied herself forever. The kind of heights she only reached with him, clinging to him, reveling in every moment of her own peak and then his, until all that was left was exhaustion and pounding pulses.

"I love you, Issa," Hutch said breathlessly.

"I love you, too," Issa responded.

Then he kissed her temple and rolled them both to their sides where only bodies spoke—melded together in perfect harmony.

And in that moment before Issa gave in to the exhaustion that was overtaking her, she knew that right there in Hutch's arms was where she belonged. That regardless of how complicated their situation, this was where she was meant to be.

With this man.

In the perfect partnership.

Forming the family they would form—part his, part hers.

Each of them stronger and better and happier together than either of them could ever be alone.

* * * * *

HEART & HOME

Heartwarming romances where love can
happen right when you least expect it.

◆ Harlequin®
SPECIAL EDITION®

COMING NEXT MONTH
AVAILABLE JANUARY 31, 2012

#2167 FORTUNE'S VALENTINE BRIDE
The Fortunes of Texas: Whirlwind Romance
Marie Ferrarella

#2168 THE RETURN OF BOWIE BRAVO
Bravo Family Ties
Christine Rimmer

#2169 JACKSON HOLE VALENTINE
Rx for Love
Cindy Kirk

#2170 A MATCH MADE BY CUPID
The Foster Brothers
Tracy Madison

#2171 ALMOST A HOMETOWN BRIDE
Helen R. Myers

#2172 HIS MOST IMPORTANT WIN
Cynthia Thomason

You can find more information on upcoming Harlequin® titles,
free excerpts and more at www.HarlequinInsideRomance.com.

HSECNM0112